JOINING THE SWIM TEAM IS CHARLIE'S WORST NIGHTMARE.

"But I don't know how to swim, sir. I can't even tread water."

"You have flippers, scales, and a tail, Mr. Drinkwater. You'll learn."

"No offense, Principal Muchnick, but I don't really want to learn."

"Do you really want to graduate from seventh grade?" Principal Muchnick smiles at me. He looks just like Jack Nicholson in *The Shining*. Only scarier.

"But sir," I plead. "A person should have the freedom to choose his or her own extracurricular activities. Shouldn't they?" I feel that dull ache you get at the bottom of your throat when you are trying to stop yourself from crying.

"What do you think this is, Drinkwater, a democracy?" Professor Muchnick bellows. "You're in seventh grade and what I say goes. Period. Now get out of here before I sign you up for the Marines." He holds the receiver up to his ear. "Willard Muchnick here. I've got some terrific news for you, Coach Grubman. Are you sitting down?"

I stagger out of his omelling Principal Muchnick's che⎯⎯⎯⎯⎯⎯⎯⎯⎯⎯⎯⎯⎯⎯⎯⎯⎯⎯⎯⎯⎯nake my way down the stairs and ⎯⎯⎯⎯⎯⎯⎯⎯⎯⎯⎯⎯⎯⎯⎯⎯⎯⎯ho runs away, screaming for his mother.

How am I going to get myself out of this mess?

OTHER BOOKS YOU MAY ENJOY

The CREATURE
FROM THE SEVENTH GRADE

SINK OR SWIM

The CREA FROM THE SINK OR SWIM

PUFFIN BOOKS
An Imprint of Penguin Group (USA)

TURF

SEVENTH GRADE

#2

by **BOB BALABAN**

illustrated by **ANDY RASH**

PUFFIN BOOKS
Published by the Penguin Group
Penguin Group (USA) LLC
375 Hudson Street
New York, New York 10014

USA * Canada * UK * Ireland * Australia
New Zealand * India * South Africa * China

penguin.com
A Penguin Random House Company

First published in the United States of America by Viking,
an imprint of Penguin Young Readers Group, 2013
Published by Puffin Books, an imprint of Penguin Young Readers Group, 2014

THE LIBRARY OF CONGRESS HAS CATALOGED THE VIKING EDITION AS FOLLOWS:
Balaban, Bob.
The creature from the seventh grade : sink or swim / by Bob Balaban ; illustrated by Andy Rash.
pages cm
Summary: "Shortly after spontaneously morphing into a giant mutant dinosaur, 12-year-old
Charlie Drinkwater discovers he's not the only creature in town"—Provided by publisher.
ISBN 978-0-670-01272-5 (hardcover)
[1. Self-acceptance—Fiction. 2. Stealing—Fiction. 3. Popularity—Fiction.
4. Middle schools—Fiction. 5. Schools—Fiction. 6. Cousins—Fiction.
7. Family life—Illinois—Fiction. 8. Humorous stories.]
I. Rash, Andy, illustrator. II. Title. III. Title: Sink or swim.
PZ7.B1793Crs 2013
[Fic]—dc23
2013010721

Puffin Books ISBN 978-0-14-242672-2

Printed in the United States of America

Book design and student planner doodles by Jim Hoover

1 3 5 7 9 10 8 6 4 2

To Miles and Henry, two terrific kids
who care about doing the right thing

—B. B.

To Jorie and Merrick,
my two favorite seventh graders

—A. R.

CONTENTS

The CREATURE
FROM THE SEVENTH GRADE
SINK OR SWIM

PROLOGUE

THE FOLLOWING IS a list of things that I was afraid of when I was in sixth grade. I hope you are sitting down because this is going to take a while. Here goes:

Swimming; standing up in front of the class and giving oral reports; the dark; mummies who come to life three thousand years after they were embalmed and decide to kill you for absolutely no reason except that they are a mummy and you aren't; Craig Dieterly, my nemesis, who is scarier than an entire army of zombies and blood-sucking vampires combined; eating liver, the most frightening food on the planet except for maybe rhubarb, the other most frightening food on the planet except for maybe tapioca pudding, which is like eating mucus with fish eyes in it only worse.

Wait. There's more:

Insects that sting you; insects that look like they *could* sting you even they don't actually have stingers (like praying mantises and dragonflies); finding yourself alone in the elevator with certain people like Amy Armstrong, the cutest girl in Stevenson Middle School and possibly the universe, and trying to have a conversation with her and getting nowhere; meteors from outer space hurtling toward earth at supersonic speed that could wipe out life as we know it. And last but not least, in case you forgot: swimming.

Now that I am in seventh grade I am learning to develop strategies to help me deal with some of the things that I was afraid of when I was younger. Like Dr. Craverly, our school psychologist, says, "We cannot always conquer our deepest fears, but if we work very hard and do exactly what our school psychologist tells us, sometimes we can turn them into our friends instead of our enemies." And sometimes we can't.

This is a story about how it's not just dreams that come true. It's nightmares, too. What you are about to hear actually happened to me. My name really is Charlie Drinkwater. I really do attend Stevenson Middle School, grades five through eight, in Decatur, Illinois. Craig Dieterly really does hate me. And no matter what your parents tell you, monsters really do exist and sometimes they even jump out at you from the bushes and try to grab on to your leg when you least expect it.

Read on if you dare.

Notes:

Ask Mom to buy
twenty more cans
of sardines for
snacks

Remember to
file claws

Argh!
AA!

Learn how
to SWIM

Don't forget
to watch
partial moon
eclipse tonight
at eleven

Ninja!

1
SOMETHING FISHY

"I CAN'T WALK Balthazar this morning, Mom," Dave pleads. "I have to get to school early for my physics makeup exam."

Balthazar looks up at my older brother with his sad brown eyes and whines. Nobody ever wants to walk him. He's a great dog, but he can't be rushed. He has to sniff every single bush, tree, and fire hydrant in the neighborhood before he'll even *think* about getting down to business.

"But it's your turn, Dave. You've got to." Mom

races around the kitchen, cleaning up the breakfast dishes. "Fred, turn off that TV this minute. You barely touched your eggs." My dad sits glued to the little TV set on the counter like he does every morning. "A balanced breakfast is the beginning of—"

"Shhh, Doris," Dad interrupts. "I'm watching something important on the news." My father slurps his coffee, shoves all of his eggs and bacon onto a piece of toast, and gulps everything down in one huge bite. "Somebody broke into Howard Dieterly's fish store this morning and stole all of his salmon."

"You'll get an ulcer if you keep eating like that, I swear." My mom turns off the TV, grabs my dad's plate, and hurries over to the sink. "Charlie, please make sure to be extra nice to Craig Dieterly at school today. I know you two don't exactly get along, but if *your* father's store ever got broken into, I'm sure Craig would be extra nice to you."

"Yeah, sure, Mom." Boy, does my mom not get it. If *my* dad's store ever got broken into, Craig Dieterly would probably throw a big party to celebrate the occasion and invite everybody in my grade except me.

"Why can't Charlie walk Balthazar?" Dave asks. "That's what little brothers are for." Dave hands Balthazar a piece of bacon under the table.

"No people food, honey," my mom orders. "Bally's stomach is still upset from the pumpkin."

That would be my jack-o'-lantern. I left it out for so long that it rotted and got pumpkin goop all over the front steps to our house, like it does every year. Balthazar scarfed down a whole bunch of it and then barfed all over the wall-to-wall carpeting in the living room. And now every time he burps it smells like Halloween all over again.

"I walked him yesterday *and* the day before, Dave," I reply. "He's your dog too, you know."

"Don't fight, kids." My mom reaches over and pats Balthazar reassuringly. "Any minute, Bally, I promise."

My dad turns the TV back on. "Quiet, everybody, they're interviewing the police. I want to listen to this."

"You can hear all about Howard Dieterly and his salmon when you're in the car on the way to work." Mom flicks off the TV again. "Go upstairs and get dressed, Fred. You can't go to the office in your pj's. And put a little speed on. Remember, you're dropping me at my appointment this morning, and I don't want to be late for it." She wipes her hands on a dish towel.

My mom runs a small catering company called Slim Pickings. She has this big meeting today with Mr. Hollabird. He owns a chain of health-food kiosks called Beautiful Bites. She's really nervous about it. She is hoping to convince him to carry her delicious new line of fat-free low-calorie desserts.

Mr. Hollabird's only son, Grady, is in my grade. He is famous for (A) getting the biggest allowance in the middle school (I am not allowed to tell you how much because my mom says it's rude to talk about other people's money) and (B) eating potato chips and Fig Newtons for lunch every single day for the last three years in a row. My mom says he only does this to torture his father.

"I'll give you three dollars and my solemn promise to walk Balthazar for the next two days if you take him out this morning." My brother pulls out his wallet before I even have a chance to reply.

"Four dollars and three days and it's a deal." I hold out my right claw. Dave shakes it gingerly. It's really sharp.

Speaking of claws: did I mention that I spontaneously morphed into an eight-and-a-half-foot tall, seven-hundred-and-fifty-pound mutant dinosaur two weeks ago during Mr. Arkady's science class? It was like *Freaky Friday*, only instead it was *Monster Monday*. I sprouted claws, flippers, and an eight-foot tail. I used to be the dorkiest kid in seventh grade. Now I'm the dorkiest lizard.

According to my mom it's genetic. Only no one else in my immediate family got the dinosaur-instead-of-teenager gene. She also says it's permanent. I'm still trying to get used to it. *Trying* is the operative word here.

"Deal!" Dave exclaims. He is out the door faster than you can say "sometimes having a big brother can lead to a positive cash flow." I throw Balthazar's leash on him and go get my coat.

"What do we always do before we leave the house in the morning, Charlie?" Mom raises her eyebrows meaningfully.

"I already made my bed, Mom," I answer hopefully. "You didn't even have to ask. Can I go now?"

"I have two words for you, Charles Drinkwater." My mom points to the bathroom. "Brush your fangs this minute and I'm not kidding."

"Do I have to, Mom? Please!" She won't even dignify the question with a response. Balthazar lies down in the middle of the floor and whimpers in protest while I brush and floss every single one of my sixty-three razor-sharp monster teeth. And *then* I take the poor dog out for his three-zillion-mile walk.

Half an hour later, I am rushing like a maniac to Stevenson Middle School. I don't want to mar my perfect attendance record. When you are the only mutant dinosaur in your grade, sneaking quietly into your classroom after the bell rings is not exactly an option.

I careen down the block, crashing through neatly piled heaps of brilliantly colored fallen leaves. I'm going so fast I nearly trip over my enormous tail. My breath comes out my long, bony snout in puffy white bursts. It's only the second week in November, but already it's threatening to snow.

A mere two weeks ago I was the skinniest kid in the entire middle school. As soon as the temperature dropped below seventy degrees my lips would turn blue and my teeth would start chattering. I had to wear mittens on top of my mittens. But now that I am a mutant dinosaur, winter weather doesn't bother me a bit.

Pretty soon I arrive at the intersection of Lonesome Lane and Cedar Street, where my two best friends, Sam Endervelt and Lucille Strang, are standing on the curb, waiting for me. "Where've you been, pal?" Sam asks when he sees me.

"We've been waiting for you forever, Charlie," Lucille chimes in.

"I had to walk Balthazar. It's a miracle I even got here."

"We figured you were out catching breakfast lizards, or whatever it is you mutant dinosaurs do every morning." Sam chuckles and tugs at the fake nose ring he always wears. He thinks it makes him look trendy or cool or something. Trust me, it doesn't. His dyed purple hair and black fingernail polish don't help much, either. He looks like Gomez from the Addams Family no matter what he does.

Sam, Lucille, and I have been walking to school together ever since second grade, when we formed a local chapter of the Junior Scientists of America and insisted on wearing our official lab coats and matching propeller beanies everywhere we went. The rest of the class decided we were off-the-charts geeky and refused to be seen in public with us ever since.

There are worse things than being the three most unpopular kids in Stevenson Middle School, grades five through eight. Only at the moment I can't think of any. My friends and I keep track of our popularity on a pretend graph we keep in our minds. Our combined score is currently minus two hundred. And getting lower every day.

"Come on, guys." Lucille looks at her watch. "First period's about to start. Let's get this show on the road." The light changes and we hustle across the street. Lucille is over six feet tall and ultra skinny. She has these unbelievably long legs. It's really hard to keep up with her.

We are across the road and halfway down the block when someone calls to us in a high, squeaky voice, "Hold your horses!"

Alice Pincus races up to us, followed by a bunch of the other popular kids in my class. The girls are called One-Upsters. They travel in a mindless pack and never hand in their homework on time. Their favorite expression is "way cool." Their favorite color is "bright and sparkly." They hang out with the popular boys, who are called Banditos.

Banditos travel in an equally mindless pack, have an average IQ of ten, and can rarely be found without their Gatorade. Their favorite hobbies are hitting people on the arm and lighting farts.

Lucille, Sam, and I belong to a clique, too. We're called Mainframes. We get good grades and teachers like us. You can always spot Mainframes in a crowd. We're the ones everybody's trying to avoid.

"Hey, Charlie!" says Rachel Klempner, one of Alice's best friends. "Let's hang together at recess." Rachel drags Larry Wykoff, her boyfriend, along like a startled poodle on a leash. To say they are inseparable is putting it mildly. If those two lovebirds are apart for more than sixty seconds they have to be given CPR.

I don't even bother to reply. Rachel Klempner is a complete and total liar. She wouldn't hang out with me if she was dying of a rattlesnake bite and I had the antidote.

"What do you guys want?" Sam asks.

"We're looking for suspects," Alice Pincus replies curtly.

"What are they suspected of?" Lucille asks.

"Bad things. Duh." Alice rolls her eyes. "We're in the middle of a crime wave, Lucille, in case you haven't noticed. Craig's dad's fish store just got broken into, and we're not going to rest until every last criminal in this town is safely behind bars." Alice Pincus may be the littlest girl in middle school, but she makes up for it with a big attitude.

"What are you going to do, Alice, arrest them with your pencil?" Lucille doesn't like Alice Pincus. The feeling is mutual.

"This is no laughing matter," Rachel Klempner warns.

"Look, Alice," I begin. "I'm really sorry Mr. Dieterly's fish store got broken into this morning, but one robbery does not a crime wave make."

"Yeah, well, for your information, Charlie, Marvin O'Connor just got robbed, too," Rachel Klempner snaps.

"Uncle Marvin? Really?" I am stunned. Marvin O'Connor is married to my mom's sister, Harriet. They're two of the nicest people in the world. They're also really strange. "Two crimes in one morning? What did the robber take?"

"A bag of your uncle's stinky old used shoes," Alice Pincus answers. "We just ran into him on our way to school. He was on his way to report the incident to the police and told us all about it. I took notes." She pulls out a little yellow pad and starts flipping through it.

"I bet you did," Lucille says drily.

"What would anybody ever want with Uncle Marvin's used shoe collection?"

"That's exactly what we were wondering, Charlie." Rachel Klempner stares at me suspiciously.

"Is Charlie's uncle okay?" Sam asks, tugging nervously at his nose ring.

"He's fine. We're not so sure about the shoes," Larry Wykoff jokes. He's the class clown. There's one in every grade. It's written in the student bylaws.

Lucille checks her watch and starts walking toward school again. The rest of the group follows her.

As we make our way down Cedar Street, the One-Upsters and Banditos are careful to keep their distance from me, Sam, and Lucille, just in case anyone notices them walking to school with us and thinks they have lost their collective minds.

"What exactly did Uncle Marvin say to you, Alice?" I duck to avoid a low-hanging branch.

"I thought you'd never ask," Alice replies. "Your uncle said he was on his way to his insurance company to have his used shoe collection appraised this morning." She peers down at her notepad and reads aloud. "Quote: 'I'm alone. The street's deserted. At approximately seven forty a.m. I hear the perpetrator's footsteps approaching from behind. I turn into an alley and try to elude the stalker. I can feel the evil pursuer's hot breath on my neck when all of a sudden a large bony hand reaches out from nowhere, grabs my shoe collection, wrenches it from my trembling fingers, and disappears into the morning mist without a trace.' End quote."

"Are you just saying this to scare the bejesus out of us, Alice Pincus?" Lucille asks. "Because if you are, you're doing an extremely good job."

I quickly add "stalkers with bony hands who pursue you down alleys" to my list of things I am afraid of. Life just keeps getting scarier.

2
SAY IT ISN'T SO

AS WE CONTINUE our walk to school, Amy Armstrong, the queen of the One-Upsters, spots us and scuttles over, fluffing her perfect blonde hair as she goes. Norm Swerling, the class snitch, tags along. "What are you people doing hanging out with *them*?" Amy points to me, Sam, and Lucille.

"Looking for eyewitnesses." Alice struggles to climb over a fallen branch lying on the sidewalk. It is nearly as tall as she is. "The perpetrator appears to have been heading in this direction. Did any of you notice an extremely tall man running toward Cedar Street and carrying a bag of old shoes this morning?" She suddenly wheels on me and points dramatically. "Where were *you* at precisely seven fifty-five a.m., Charlie Drinkwater?"

"I was leaving my house and heading down Lonesome Lane. What are you getting at?"

"Are you absolutely certain?" Alice Pincus persists. "Think hard. Exactly where were you?"

"Exactly where he always is at seven fifty-five every school morning," Lucille interrupts. "On his way to school. Like every other normal person in the entire seventh grade."

"Charlie Drinkwater, normal?" Amy Armstrong snorts. "That's a hoot."

"That's not nice!" Sam snaps.

"I don't intend it to be," Amy replies.

"Do you swear on the life of your dog that you didn't see a tall man carrying a big bag of—" Alice Pincus begins.

"Get serious, people. Charlie doesn't have to swear on anything," Lucille says. "He isn't a liar. He's the most decent, trustworthy person in the entire middle school. Which is a whole lot more than I can say for the rest of you."

"*Trustworthy?*" Alice Pincus shrieks. "That's a laugh. Are you trying to tell me you don't think he had anything to do with the break-in at Craig Dieterly's father's fish store?" Alice Pincus tucks her notepad back into her waistband and puts her tiny hands on her even tinier waist.

"I'm not *trying* to tell you. I'M TELLING YOU!" Lucille practically shouts. "HE DIDN'T!"

"I was home sleeping," I protest. "I didn't do anything. Ask my parents. Ask my brother. Ask my dog. Why would I lie about a thing like that?"

"Oh, come off it, Drinkwater." Amy Armstrong sighs. "Everybody in town thinks you did it."

"But that's ridiculous! Why would I steal my uncle's old shoes? I may be large and green and scaly, but that doesn't automatically make me a thief."

"Oh yeah?" Amy Armstrong counters. "Then tell me this: who else could carry away that much salmon?"

"He even smells like salmon," Norm Swerling adds.

"Just because I *could* have done it doesn't mean I actually did it!" Argh! I hate being wrongfully accused. I don't even like being *rightfully* accused all that much.

"Maybe it wasn't your idea," Alice Pincus suggests.

"Maybe you only helped break the door down. Maybe you were just an accessory before the fact. But you had something to do with it. I'd bet my life on it. Frankly I didn't even trust you all that much when you were human, Charlie Drinkwater."

With that, Alice Pincus marches away. Her One-Upster and Bandito friends chase after her quicker than you can say "certain very short people have been watching too many crime shows on TV lately."

"That is so unfair I can't stand it!" Lucille exclaims.

"Double ditto," Sam says.

My friends and I take the shortcut through the ravine and hightail it to school. I try not to trip over my enormous flippers. We mutant dinosaurs prefer the plains. We don't do well with hills and valleys.

"We've got a real mystery on our hands, guys!" Sam exclaims. "With a perp and a victim and unusual circumstances and everything!" Sam can barely catch his breath. "I wonder if the robber who stole Charlie's uncle's shoes is the same guy who broke into Mr. Dieterly's fish store?"

"I wonder if it's somebody we know," Lucille adds. "Wouldn't that be creepy?"

"Yeah!" I say. "Just like in *House of Wax* when Professor Henry Jarrod stalks the young and beautiful Sue

Allen, and after he catches her he dips her in a vat of boiling hot wax and sticks her in his creepy exhibit of wax-coated corpses, and nobody realizes the dead woman is right under everybody's nose."

"Exactly like in *House of Wax*," Sam says. "Only this *really happened*! And whoever did it is still *on the loose*!"

My friends and I have seen *Wax*, as we like to call it, four and a half times. (The last time we watched it Balthazar ate a bowl of popcorn and threw up all over the couch. We had to stop in the middle to clean up the mess.) Our version of choice is the original, starring Vincent Price. Not the remake, starring Paris Hilton, which gets a minus ten on our fear-o-meter.

The three of us love being scared. We will watch anything that gets the hairs on our necks to stand up. Of course, I don't exactly have hairs on my neck anymore. I have scales. And I couldn't get them to stand up if King Kong walked into my room carrying Jack the Ripper on his shoulders.

"We're here, guys." Sam points to the herd of wild animals otherwise known as the Stevenson Middle School student body, and we elbow our way across the courtyard and climb the big stone steps that lead to the lobby. My eight-foot tail barely makes it through the heavy metal front door before it slams behind us.

The warning bell for first period rings. We've got Mr. Arkady's science class in exactly sixty seconds.

Mr. Arkady is my favorite teacher, and not just because he has pointy teeth, wears a black cape, and looks exactly like Dracula. But it helps.

I like Mr. Arkady because if you ever have a problem you can always go to him for advice and he never makes you feel like you're stupid. Unfortunately, he takes off for lateness. We make a mad dash for the third floor.

"What's hangin', slimy flipper boy?" Craig Dieterly, king of the Banditos, says as he spots me hauling my seven-hundred-and-fifty-pound body up the stairs. He has been making my life miserable ever since we started pre-K together, eight long years ago. "Eat any disgusting insects lately?" He cheerfully punches me so hard in what passes for my arm that I could cry, only I would never give him the satisfaction. I turn around and glare right at him. But mutant dinosaurs basically always look like they are glaring, so I doubt if Craig Dieterly even notices.

"Sticks and stones may break my bones, but names will never hurt me." The second it is out of my mouth I regret it.

"That is so third grade it's pathetic, Drinkwater."
Craig Dieterly shoves me against the railing.

"Hey, watch it, Dieterly," Lucille says angrily.

"Why don't you go pick on someone else for a change?" Sam suggests.

"Fat chance," he growls at Sam. He grabs my neck in his big beefy hands and gets right in my face. "I'm *glad* you broke into my dad's store. Know why, Turtle Breath?"

I shake my head, unable to speak.

"Because when they prove you did it, you will get into so much trouble you'll wish you had never been born. I'm sick and tired of you making the rest of us look bad with your dumb four-point-six average and your sucky extra credit papers. It's time somebody made you pay for all the misery you cause for the rest of us."

Craig Dieterly's two Neanderthal-sized friends, Dirk and Dack Schlissel, join us on the stairs. They are famous for two things: having the lowest combined grade point average in the history of seventh grade, and picking their noses when they think nobody is looking.

"Hey, Dieterly, what do you get when you cross a mutant dinosaur with the geekiest kid in seventh grade?" one of them asks.

"I give up," Craig Dieterly replies. "What do you get?"

"Sick to your stomach!" the other one answers. The Schlissel twins and Craig Dieterly howl with laughter and race up the stairs three at a time.

"What kind of trouble do you think I could get in, guys?" I ask.

"Don't even think about it," Lucille says firmly.

"You're innocent, pal," Sam adds. "Nothing's going to happen to you."

As my friends and I approach the classroom, I notice Mr. Arkady waiting in the hallway, tapping one of his long, pointy velvet slippers and wagging his bony finger at me. "Follow me, Mr. Drinkvater," he commands ominously.

"Can we come, too?" Lucille asks.

"No." Mr. Arkady doesn't say another word. He just marches me up the stairs toward the principal's office. I tuck my enormous tail firmly between my powerful haunches and wonder what on earth I've done this time.

3

IT'S THE PRINCIPAL OF THE THING

"WHY'D YOU DO IT, Drinkwater?" Principal Muchnick growls the second I enter his majestic, wood-paneled, book-lined office.

I try hard not to sneeze as his cologne hits my sensitive snout like a ton of bricks. Principal Muchnick must have a closet filled with the stuff. He never smells the same way twice. Last Friday he smelled like dirty socks and vinaigrette. Today he smells like cheap cigars and Elmer's glue. Ever since I became a creature, I can basically detect a molecule of cinnamon from two miles away.

This is more than I can handle. I hold my claws over my nostrils and try not to gag.

"Why'd I do what, sir?" I ask.

"You know perfectly well what I'm talking about." Principal Muchnick glares at me.

Dr. Craverly, the school psychologist, stands next to him, looking concerned. Concerned is Dr. Craverly's main look. His other look is incompetent.

"Someone stole thirty-two loaves of freshly baked sourdough bread from the cafeteria this morning, Charlie," Craverly says. "They had to scale a fifteen-foot brick wall and break down a steel door to do it. You have to admit it looks pretty—"

"It wasn't me, I swear," I interrupt. "I was home all morning. Ask anybody. It couldn't have been me." Sheesh. In my whole life I have never been suspected of so many things in such a short amount of time.

"Tell it to the judge, Drinkwater." When Principal Muchnick fixes his penetrating gaze on you, it's like a laser beam. You can practically feel it burning into your skin. (Or scales, in my particular case.)

"Have a little patience, Willard," Dr. Craverly says. "The boy's been through a lot."

If my first name was Willard, you'd have to pull off my fingernails to get me to admit it. If I had fingernails. My middle name is even worse. It's Elmer, and if you ever tell anybody I will deny it, so don't even think about it.

"I don't care if he's been to hell and back, Craverly," Principal Muchnick says. "I will not tolerate antisocial behavior in this school for one instant." He turns abruptly and aims his beady little eyes right at me. "Do you read me loud and clear, Mr. Drinkwater?"

Principal Muchnick has had it in for me ever since he made football mandatory for all fifth-grade boys and I organized a school-wide protest. It didn't work, but Principal Muchnick never forgot.

"Yes, sir."

"Then why did you force your way into the cafeteria and steal thirty-two loaves of freshly baked sourdough bread?" Principal Muchnick's chubby red face is getting rounder and rosier by the second. He looks like a balloon that's about to pop.

"I didn't," I reply nervously. "I swear. I'm innocent. I don't even like sourdough bread. I prefer seeded rye."

"Are you seriously going to stand there and tell me someone else in this town was able to scale a fifteen-foot brick wall and break down a steel door with his bare hands?" Principal Muchnick runs his pudgy fingers through his oily black hair.

"Yes, sir." I shift nervously from one flipper to the other.

Doc Craverly looks at me and shakes his head sadly. "Adolescents," he murmurs. "One minute they're helping little old ladies across the street. The next they're pushing them into it."

"What in the Sam Hill is that supposed to mean, Craverly?" Principal Muchnick screams at the psychologist. "Nobody's pushing any little old ladies into the street."

Doc Craverly starts to tremble. "Raging ha . . . ha . . . hormones . . . Willard," he stammers. "They can turn the nicest ka . . . ka . . . kid into a frustrated and belligerent fugitive from ja . . . ja . . . justice just like that!" Doctor Craverly tries to snap his fingers for emphasis, but they're so drenched with sweat they slide off each other silently.

"You're the doctor in the house," Muchnick roars. "What do you suggest we do about this?"

"I suggest Charlie start participating in a team sport

immediately," Doctor Craverly says meekly. "It'll do him a world of ga . . . ga . . . ga . . . good."

"That's the stupidest thing I ever heard in my life!" Principal Muchnick snorts.

"I ba . . . ba . . . beg to da . . . da . . . differ," Doc Craverly stammers. He is not much for confrontations.

"Why?" Principal Muchnick demands. "This better be good, Craverly." Doc Craverly gulps air like a dying guppy while his mouth silently forms words. "Pull yourself together, man," Principal Muchnick barks. "You are a trained professional in the field of mental health."

Doc Craverly takes a deep breath and steadies himself, and the words come tumbling out. "The rebellious adolescent often masks insecurity by acting out in a futile attempt to establish a stronger sense of his or her own identity. Joining a team has been known to engender the feeling of order and discipline so often lacking in the unruly youngster, encouraging self-esteem while bolstering the confidence necessary to become a productive member of one's own community." Doc Craverly wipes away perspiration from his forehead with his sleeve.

"I have no idea what you just said, but I like it, Craverly. Congratulations, Drinkwater, you're joining a team," Principal Muchnick says. "And you will stay on it until you stop acting out in this antisocial manner. Got it?"

I have never been much of a team player. In third grade I signed up for intramural volleyball. The first day we played, all seventeen other members of the team signed a petition saying that if I remained on it, they were quitting. I missed the ball every time it came near me. The one time I hit it back, I smacked Amy Armstrong in the head so hard she had to be sent home.

I manage to come out with a feeble, "What team am I joining, sir?"

"I'm not sure." Principal Muchnick shuts his eyes. He concentrates intensely. A moment later they snap open and he beams at me. "The swimming team. It's perfect!"

I am not joining the swimming team. Never. Ever. I don't care if they throw me in jail and feed me stale bread crumbs for the rest of my life. I feel like screaming *Noooooo* at the top of my lungs.

But what actually comes out is, "I'd rather not, sir."

"Nonsense," Principal Muchnick replies. "We've finished last in three meets out of four, and we swim against our archrivals, the Carbondale Catfish, on Friday. You're just the thing we need to lift the Stevenson Sardines out of their slump. An actual fish. I can just picture the headline: 'Sardines Drown Catfish in Virtuoso Swimming Display.' We'll be on our way to the division finals in no time!"

"Technically speaking, I'm not a fish, sir. I'm a mutant dinosaur." I am starting to panic.

"Technically speaking, I wouldn't care if you were an armadillo," Principal Muchnick snaps. "Whatever you *were*, you're a Sardine now, Drinkwater. Don't try to wriggle out of it." Principal Muchnick laughs at his stupid joke. "You start practice tomorrow after school." He returns to his desk. "Craverly, you go locate the appropriate parental approval forms while I call Coach Grubman and give him the good news." He grabs the phone.

"But I don't know how to swim, sir. I can't even tread water."

"You have flippers, scales, and a tail, Mr. Drinkwater. You'll learn."

"No offense, Principal Muchnick, but I don't really want to learn."

"Do you really want to graduate from seventh

grade?" Principal Muchnick smiles at me. He looks just like Jack Nicholson in *The Shining*. Only scarier.

"But sir," I plead. "A person should have the freedom to choose his or her own extracurricular activities. Shouldn't they?" I feel that dull ache you get at the bottom of your throat when you are trying to stop yourself from crying.

"What do you think this is, Drinkwater, a democracy?" Professor Muchnick bellows. "You're in seventh grade and what I say goes. Period. Now get out of here before I sign you up for the Marines." He holds the receiver up to his ear. "Willard Muchnick here. I've got some terrific news for you, Coach Grubman. Are you sitting down?"

I stagger out of his office. I am so light-headed from smelling Principal Muchnick's cheap cologne that I stumble as I make my way down the stairs and nearly flatten a fifth grader, who runs away, screaming for his mother.

How am I going to get myself out of this mess?

4
FOLLOW THE YELLOW BRICK ROAD

"MAYBE YOU'LL *LIKE* being on the swimming team," Sam says. "You never know until you try it."

"Fat chance," I mutter.

Sam and Lucille and I are on our way to my house after school. My mom is making us dinner tonight. We're also going to do our homework, learn ten vocabulary words, and watch a scary movie if there's time left over.

We take the shortcut past Devil's Hill and double back around Crater Lake, the deepest body of water in southern Illinois. It was formed when a giant meteor crashed to earth at the end of the Cretaceous period, over sixty-five million years ago, wiping out most of the planet's dinosaur population.

At that point, according to my mom, a few of my distant dinosaur ancestors mutated and swam to safety at the bottom of lake. Many millions of years later, my Mom's mom, a mutant dinosaur named Nana Wallabird, crawled out of the bottom of the lake and onto dry land, and married Grampa, a human. And that's how I eventually became scaly old me.

"Give it a chance," Sam says. "Being on a team can be a fun and rewarding experience." He pulls his collar up around his neck as a few wispy flakes of snow begin to whirl around our heads.

"If you think being on a team is so wonderful, why don't *you* join one?" I ask.

"I've been on the chess team for years," Sam answers.

"They just *call* it a team," I say. "Everyone knows it's really a club, Sam. Come on. And for your information, there are eight zillion good reasons I don't want to be on the swimming team, starting with they make you go into the deep end and I could drown."

"You're taller than the deep end, Charlie," Sam

chides. "I strongly doubt that you would drown."

"A person could drown in five inches of water if they hit their head on the side of the pool and got knocked unconscious," I reply. "It happens every day."

We veer left at the fork at Willow Hollow Road and turn right onto Maple Drive. Only six more blocks to 442 Lonesome Lane. I can smell my mom's delicious cooking from here.

"Let me get this straight," Sam begins. "Muchnick made you join the swimming team because he thinks you stole his sourdough bread?"

"In a nutshell, yes," I reply.

"That doesn't make any sense!" Lucille exclaims.

"Since when did Principal Muchnick ever make any sense?" I say. "Doc Craverly thinks that if I join a team I'll feel more productive and improve my self-image and stop stealing stuff." I duck to avoid getting hit in the head by a branch.

"But you're not a thief," Sam reasons. "You are so innocent it hurts."

"Tell it to Craverly, Sam," I say. "Quick. Before I drown."

"All we have to do is apprehend the *real* thief," Sam

explains. "And when we do, everybody will know you didn't do anything bad, and you won't have to be on the swimming team. Kaboom."

"How come you're so sure there weren't three thieves?" Lucille asks. "One for each crime."

"Intuition," Sam answers. "Pure and simple. There hasn't been a robbery in our neighborhood for as long as I can remember. And now suddenly three different people decide to turn criminal all in one morning?" Sam shakes his head. "Doesn't make sense. The one-perp theory is much more likely." Sam abruptly makes a left turn onto Cedar Street.

"Where are you going, Sam?" Lucille asks. "Charlie's house is that way." She points in the other direction.

"We're going to Mr. Dieterly's fish store to search for clues," Sam says. "While they're still fresh."

We link arms and march into town together. I am so tall I have to stoop down to reach. I don't mind. Clearing my good name and getting me off the swimming team is my idea of a great way to spend an afternoon. Soon we reach Dieterly's Delectable Denizens of the Deep, site of this morning's infamous Salmon Robbery.

Joe Jefferson, daytime anchor for W-H-A-T, the

local news channel, spots us and rushes over with his crew to do an impromptu interview. He smooths his already perfectly arranged wavy brown hair. While one assistant applies powder to his forehead, the other brushes away invisible pieces of lint from his broad shoulders.

"Tell the audience at home, kids, do you have any idea who might have committed this dreadful crime?" Joe Jefferson intones in his deep and professionally phony announcer voice. "What about you, young . . . uh. Young . . . uh . . ." He is staring at me intently, trying to figure out what to call me. He pokes his microphone in what passes for my face. "Who do you think did it?"

I look at Lucille, dumbfounded. Sam takes over the role of designated spokesperson for our little group. "We don't know anything about any robberies. We were out enjoying the beautiful autumn weather, and we just wandered over to buy some fish. For dinner. Because we love fish. Don't we?"

"Yes, we do." Lucille jumps right in. "Fish is both healthy and delicious. It's just about our favorite food." She smiles. "It's easily digestible and goes especially well with a green vegetable or any member of the pasta family, and um—"

Lucille stops abruptly because Sam has just given her a brisk kick in the shins.

"You actually appear to *be* a fish, young uh . . . young . . . uh . . ." Joe Jefferson still cannot think of what to call me. He edges his microphone closer, careful not to get his fingers anywhere near my fangs.

"I'm not really a fish," I reply. "I'm a mutant amphibious vertebrate." I find myself feeling rather excited to be making my first TV appearance, but I resist the opportunity to try out a few jokes. Instead I stick to the facts. "It's a common mistake," I explain. "Most laymen are unaware of the proper kingdom, phylum, class, order, family, genus, and species of even the most ordinary of creatures. And I could hardly be considered ordinary."

Poor Joe Jefferson is left utterly speechless by my explanation. After several uncomfortable moments he manages to pull himself together and looks back at the camera, smiling broadly. "That's a real first, folks. A fish going to a fish store to buy fish. Don't remember ever seeing that before." His smile slowly fades, and his eyes glaze over as he stops talking altogether.

"If you'll excuse us, we better get going," Sam says, practically pushing me toward the entrance to the store.

"Stop acting like an idiot and get in there, Charlie," he whispers.

"Nice chatting with you, Mr. Jefferson." Lucille smiles uncomfortably. She follows close on our heels as an assistant mops up a few uncharacteristic beads of sweat from Mr. Jefferson's forehead.

"So?" I whisper once we are inside the fish store. "What are we supposed to do now?"

"We look unobtrusive, Charlie," Lucille whispers in return. "You go distract Mr. Dieterly while Sam and I talk to possible witnesses and dust for fingerprints."

"That sounds like a good plan," I reply quietly. "Everybody has fingerprints. Except, of course, people with claws. And there aren't a lot of those running around these days." I chuckle softly while Sam and Lucille start nosing around the store.

I am feeling pretty optimistic. My friends are smart. In a few minutes they will probably solve the crime, and then I can relax and forget about drowning once and for all.

I saunter over to the counter, where Mr. Dieterly, a meek-looking little man with glasses and a pencil-thin mustache, is in the process of wrapping up a bunch of jumbo shrimp for my neighbor Mrs. Pagliuso. Mr. Dieterly doesn't look like the father of the biggest bully in middle school. With the tip of my claw, I spear a number from the ticket machine on the wall, and then I wait in line. Those shrimp sure do look tasty. I concentrate on not drooling all over the counter.

Mrs. Pagliuso watches closely to make sure Mr. Dieterly isn't throwing in any undersized shrimp. He sees me waiting in line and shakes his head. He gives a little nod to the back of the store, and Mrs. Dieterly, an imposing-looking woman with arms like the Incredible Hulk, quickly emerges from the office carrying a baseball bat. If you put Craig Dieterly in a dress and a long gray wig and didn't look too closely, you'd swear it was Mrs. Dieterly. Only not as scary. Let me put it this way: you don't have to be a genius to see what side of his family Craig Dieterly takes after.

Mrs. Dieterly sidles over to me. "I've got my eye on you, so don't try anything funny," she says under her breath. "Stay away from the salmon . . . or else." She waves her bat menacingly.

C'mon, guys, do I really look like someone who would break into a fish store and consume an entire container full of wild Norwegian Salmon? In a heartbeat. But that doesn't mean I did it.

Lucille drops some loose change on the floor near the smashed window. Sam kneels to help her pick it up. I can see him searching the ground for hairs or fibers or anything else that might belong to the suspect.

Lucille reaches into her backpack and takes out the fingerprint kit that all Junior Scientists of America in good standing carry with them everywhere. She casually takes a few imprints from the window ledge.

Let them laugh. We Junior Scientists of America know what it means to be prepared. And it's certainly coming in handy today.

"What can I do for you?" Mr. Dieterly asks when I place my ticket on the counter. I wouldn't say that he is being polite. *Civil* would be more like it. I have been so busy watching Sam and Lucille that for a second I forget why I am standing in line. "Your order," he snaps. "What is it? I don't have all day."

"I'd like six soft-shell crabs and a small container of tartar sauce on the side, please."

Mr. Dieterly is pretty fast. Sam and Lucille are still looking for clues when he finishes assembling my order.

Just as he's about to weigh it, I come out with a sudden, "Those crabs look a little undernourished to me. What do you think?"

"They look perfectly fine to me, kid," he says gruffly. As he shoves the crabs into a plastic bag, he glances over at his terrifying wife, who moves discreetly closer to where I am standing. But I can't leave yet. I still need to buy more time for my friends' sleuthing.

"I don't know," I say. "My mom told me to get the biggest ones I could find, and those don't look all that big. Do you have Alaskan king crab on your menu today? That's bigger than regular crab, isn't it?" I can see that Mrs. Dieterly is about to lose her temper, and I would really prefer to avoid getting hit in the head with a baseball bat, so I wrap up my subterfuge with a quick, "On second thought, I think I'll come back another day if that's all right with you." And then I start for the door. "Let's get going, guys," I say quietly to Sam and Lucille.

Mrs. Dieterly follows us out and plants herself in the doorway, patting her baseball bat and looking like she wouldn't think twice about smashing it over my head if we decided to return.

"Did you find what we were looking for?" I ask eagerly once we're out of earshot

"We have some preliminary findings," Lucille reports. "But nothing conclusive." We turn right at the fork onto Willow Hollow Road. We'll be home in less than ten minutes. I'm starving, but even more than that, I am eager to find out who the real culprit is.

"It's like this, Charlie," Sam begins. I can tell Sam is getting nervous because he won't stop tugging at his nose ring. "When Mr. Dieterly swept up this morning, he must have been in a real hurry to open the store, because he didn't do a very thorough job. He left behind lots of evidence."

"That's good," I say. "What did you find?"

"Well, the first thing we noticed was the unusual pattern of the stress fractures along the plaster wall surrounding the window." Lucille bites her lip. "Which, in our opinion, indicates multiple points of impact on entry."

Sam picks up where Lucille leaves off. "And then of course we observed the lack of consistency to the trajectory of the various bits of broken glass we found on the floor near the window." Sam's fake nose ring has come completely undone and looks like it could fall off his nose at any second.

"Which tends to rule out the use of a single blunt instrument," Lucille adds.

"So how'd he get in?" I ask.

Sam wraps his scarf tightly around his neck. The wind is really starting to pick up. "Our guess is the intruder used a part of his body."

"The guy probably just kicked in the window, right?" I stumble over a fallen branch and nearly fall flat on what passes for my face.

"Why are you so sure it's a guy?" Lucille asks. "Girls can be hardened criminals, too, if they want to be."

"Sure," Sam answers, "but eighty percent of all breaking and entering is done by males between the ages of seventeen and thirty. Women account for less than twelve percent of violent crime. Chapter five in the *Junior Scientists of America Crime-Stoppers* textbook."

"Of course!" Lucille says. "Now I remember."

"Anyway, the guy didn't use his feet," Sam explains. "The evidence suggests a higher point of impact. We think the thief used his hands to break the window. Only . . ." Sam sighs and shrugs his shoulders.

"What is it, Sam?' I ask.

"Only we couldn't find any fingerprints."

"He was probably wearing gloves," I say. We turn left onto Maple Drive and take a shortcut through the small deserted wooded section that backs up onto Lonesome Lane. The sky is growing darker by the second. I walk a little faster. "Wouldn't that have been the logical thing to do?"

"Absolutely," Lucille says. "Only based on the evidence collected, we don't think the intruder was wearing gloves."

"Well, maybe he wiped off his fingerprints." I am clutching at straws. And not coming up with any.

Lucille nods her head. "That's what we assumed, until we noticed a broken clock near the door. It got hit by a shard of broken glass and stopped ticking at exactly seven twelve. Mr. Dieterly opens up his store every morning at seven thirty. It says so on the door."

"We don't think the thief would have had enough time to grab all that salmon and then go around wiping off his fingerprints without running into Mr. Dieterly," Sam adds.

"Whoever broke into that store didn't leave any fingerprints, Charlie," Lucille says quietly but firmly. "Because they didn't have any to leave."

"What are you saying?" I ask.

"Whoever or whatever broke into that store doesn't appear to be human," Lucille admits.

"I'm the only nonhuman around here, and we know *I* certainly didn't do it." I wring my claws in frustration. "Because I was with *you*!"

"What if . . ." Lucille begins. "And this is only a possibility . . . but what if there's another one of you living in an alternate universe somewhere, Charlie. And you're not aware of each other. And the one you're not aware of is a thief."

"Earth to Lucille," Sam intones. "Earth to Lucille . . . come in please . . . a flesh-eating virus appears be devouring your brain . . . earth to Lucille . . ."

"Well then *you* come up with an explanation, Sam Endervelt, because I can't think of anything else!" Lucille picks up a rock and hurls it at a nearby tree. "Anyway, I only said it was a possibility."

"There's got to be a perfectly reasonable explanation," Sam says. "Only I can't seem to think of one either."

"It's starting to look like I'll be stuck on the swimming team for the rest of my life." I shake my head sadly. "How are the police ever going to apprehend someone who doesn't exist?"

Sam pulls at his nose ring so hard it flies off and lands on the sidewalk. He grabs for it and puts it back into place before you can say "my two best friends are both crazy and I hope it's only a temporary condition."

Suddenly the sound of nearby footsteps crashing through the underbrush sends Sam, Lucille, and me jumping about a mile into the air.

"What was that?" Lucille whispers.

"It's probably a raccoon," Sam says. "Mr. Arkady says they're harmless unless you threaten their young."

"Quiet," Lucille urges in a hushed tone. She gets down on her knees and presses her ear to the ground. It's an old Native American trick we learned in Mr. Arkady's science class last year. Sounds travel faster through a conducting medium such as water or earth. "Get down, everybody. Whatever it is, it's getting closer."

I try to join Lucille and Sam, but it's hard to get my neck low enough to put my earflap to the ground. Plus I get a terrible cramp in my bulging thigh and have to stifle a scream of pain as I leap up and hop around massaging my leg with both claws.

"Whatever it is seems to have stopped," Lucille announces.

"It probably knows we're listening," Sam says.

Getting scared out of your wits when you're home watching the Mummy light his tana leaves on the television set in your den is one thing. But actually being afraid in your real life is not my cup of tea. And you don't have to put your earflaps to the ground to hear the unworldly shriek that suddenly emerges from the wooded thicket just ahead of us.

"I would say that was either the hideous cry of a banshee foretelling an imminent death, or a werewolf howling at the rising moon." Sam points a stubby finger at the faintly glowing moon peeking out through the clouds overhead. "I think I'll go with werewolf."

"That's great. I feel so much better now," Lucille whispers. "Thanks a lot."

"Would you mind keeping your overactive imagination to yourself there for a minute, Sam?" I say.

The three of us huddle closely together, too frightened to move, as we wait for the howling to stop. At last we hear something clomping away through the underbrush. The sounds get fainter and fainter until at last we get up the courage to speak. "It was probably a raccoon after all," Sam suggests weakly.

"Yeah," I agree halfheartedly. "Probably." I feel like calling my parents and begging them to come get us. But now that I am twelve I have to at least *pretend* not to be a whiny little baby.

We get up from the cold, wet ground, and scrape the mud from our school shoes with twigs. And then we make a mad dash for 442 Lonesome Lane and the safety of my cozy, warm, werewolf-free kitchen.

5

FOOD, GLORIOUS FOOD

"I DON'T WANT you kids going out after dark by yourselves for a while," my mom says to Lucille, Sam, and me, putting on her apron. "Your poor uncle Marvin is still recovering from the shock of his used shoe robbery. It isn't safe out there. Not with that thief on the loose." A worried look crosses my mom's face. "Actually, Principal Muchnick stopped by this afternoon." She takes a pan of freshly baked hummus puffs out of the oven.

"He did?" I try not to sound concerned. "What did he want, Mom?"

"He asked me a lot of questions about your where-abouts this morning, honey. I told him there was no way you could have broken into school. But he was awfully persistent." She places the tray on a trivet on the table. "Careful, kids. They're hot." My mom comes up to me and gives me a big hug. "It must be terrible to have people going around thinking you did something you didn't do."

"It's not my favorite thing." I sigh.

"Dig in, kids." We don't need to be asked twice.

I spear a few of the delicious puffs with the tip of my long pointy tongue. "These are great, Mom. What do you call them?"

"Crispy Hummus Dreams, sweetie." She hums to herself as she starts arranging her mixing bowls. "Why don't you try one, Sam?"

"Don't mind if I do." Sam grabs a fistful of puffs and shoves them into his mouth until big round cheeks bulge out like a squirrel carrying around too many nuts.

"How'd your big meeting go this morning, Mom?" I ask.

"What meeting, Mrs. Drinkwater?" Lucille polishes off a Crispy Hummus Dream and reaches for another one.

"I met with Mr. Hollabird over at Beautiful Bites." My mom wipes invisible crumbs from her apron. "He invited me to make my six favorite healthy desserts and bring them to the charity bake-off his company is sponsoring the week after next. The winner gets a one-year contract and a thousand-dollar advance."

"You'll be Martha Stewart in no time, Mrs. Drinkwater!" Lucille exclaims.

"I don't know about that, Lucille, honey. Alice's mom, Sally Pincus, will be competing, too, and I'm a little concerned about it." My mom reties the bow on her apron. "If she submits her low-fat vegan pineapple upside-down cake with coconut drizzle frosting and vanilla pot de crème, my goose is cooked. No one works with tofu the way that woman does. It's uncanny."

"My money's on you, Mom." I spear a few more of those delicious hummus puffs with my gigantic tongue.

Dave comes racing into the kitchen, carrying a football under his arm. "Practice was great! I scored three touchdowns and two field goals and completed five lateral passes. Catch!" He suddenly hurls the football right at me with all his might. It hits me smack in the stomach before dropping to the floor and rolling under the table.

I am the worst catch in the history of catching.

My brother grabs the last remaining Crispy Hummus Dream and pops it into his mouth. "These are great, Mom. What's in 'em?" Dave asks.

"Love, honey. Lots of love." She brings the empty platter to the sink. "Everybody out of the kitchen this minute. I haven't even started dinner, and your father will be home soon. Shoo."

While my mom gets supper ready, Sam and Lucille and I sit in the den, learning ten new words from Wilfred Funk and Norman Lewis's book *30 Days to a More Powerful Vocabulary*, while we watch *The Raven*.

"Tawdry," Sam announces.

"Cheap or gaudy," I respond. "Overly decorated. In poor taste."

"Very good, Charlie. Use it in a sentence, Lucille," Sam orders.

"Amy Armstrong looked *tawdry* when she showed up for English class wearing false eyelashes, a fake diamond tiara, and her middle school prom dress."

Sam and I laugh. If her mother would let her that is exactly what Amy Armstrong would wear to school every day of the week.

Sam buries his head in the book while Lucille and I watch the movie. *The Raven* stars Boris Karloff as Edmond Bateman, a disfigured escaped murderer, and Bela Lugosi as Dr. Richard Vollin, a mad surgical genius with a torture chamber in his basement. We're just at the part where Doctor Vollin saves the life of the beautiful ballet dancer, played by Irene Ware, after she has been in a horribly disfiguring car accident.

The Raven is possibly the scariest movie in the history of scary movies. I do not recommend watching it (A) after midnight; (B) if you are alone; or (C) at all, if watching a movie in which an insane surgeon cuts off people's faces and then puts the poor faceless creatures into a giant box and squishes them to death makes you want to hide under your bed and never come out.

Sam looks up from the book. "Something tells me there's someone else running around Decatur making everybody think you're committing those crimes."

"Do you think Craig Dieterly is doing it to get me in trouble?" I ask.

"I don't know." Sam scratches his dark purple hair and plays with his nose ring. "All I know is it's a mystery. And I love a good mystery."

Just then Balthazar woofs excitedly as my dad strides through the front door. "I'm hoooome everybody." He tosses his scarf and his overcoat onto the little bench in the hallway. "What smells so good?"

"Suppertime, guys!" Mom calls. Dave rockets down the stairs, and my friends and I run into the dining room, take our places at the table, and dig in. "Everybody choose one new and interesting thing that happened to them today and tell it to the table. Let's start with—"

My mom doesn't even get a chance to finish her sentence when Dave blurts out, "Charlie's on the swimming team as of this morning. Coach Grubman told us all about it at football practice."

"I know, sweetie," my mom says. "Principal Muchnick told us all about it."

"Does that qualify?" Dave asks. He hands me a platter of vegetarian steak.

"It sure does," my dad replies. "It's new and interesting, and it happened to somebody."

"Unfortunately," I say, "the somebody it happened to will probably drown as a result. Anybody want more fake food?"

"You won't drown, sweetie," Mom says cheerfully.

"You have built-in flippers. You're amphibious. You'll be a great asset to the swimming team. And we call vegetarian steak *real* food where I come from, honey."

"I wouldn't call not knowing how to swim a great asset to the swimming team, Mom," I say.

"You'll just have to learn!" Dad reaches for the platter. "Remember, son, nothing's impossible."

"That's what my mom always says!" Sam exclaims.

"I bet your inner athlete is hiding inside those big green scales, just waiting for a chance to come out," Dave adds. My brother is a regular cheerleader. You can practically see him jumping around and waving pom-poms as he speaks.

"Anybody else feel like sharing?" Mom asks. She hands my dad a homemade sweet potato pie.

"Why don't you tell Dave about the new and interesting thing that happened to *you* today, Doris?" my dad says proudly.

"Mom's going to be in a bake-off and win a thousand dollars and become a famous chef and get her own show on the Food Network," I announce.

"That's fantastic, Mom." Dave is slurping down his soup so fast he's nearly finished his bowl.

"Let's not get ahead of ourselves. I'm going to be competing against real professionals." She gets up from the table and goes into the kitchen.

"Watch that negativity, Mom," Dave calls. "You have to start talking like a winner if you want to be one. Take it from me. I know a little something about the subject."

My brother has been on thirty zillion winning teams. He plays every sport known to man, and some you have never even heard of. Like underwater tennis and competitive burping. He puts his hands to his mouth like a megaphone and practically shouts: "Message to Charlie and Mom: *if you want to win, think positive*. It really works."

"Mom, when you're rich and famous, will you still make us lunch every day?" I ask.

"Maybe. If you're very, very nice to me." My mom hangs up her apron and takes her place back at the head of the table. "Charlie, when you win the big swimming race and they pin the blue ribbon on your bathing suit, will you remember to thank your friends and your family who supported and encouraged you, even on your darkest days?"

"Like that's ever going to happen," I say.

"Say, that reminds me." My mom reaches into her pocket and pulls out the little pad she keeps in there in case of sudden inspiration. "I'm going to have to make you swim trunks tonight." She pulls out a small mechanical pencil and starts sketching something that looks an awful lot like lederhosen. You know, those funny-looking shorts that Swiss yodelers wear when they go mountain climbing. "You can't very well go swimming in your birthday suit, Charlie. What would everybody think?"

"They'd think he was pretty strange, Mrs. D.," Sam says, digging into his salad. "But come to think of it, everybody already does."

By the time supper's over, the table looks like a swarm of locusts has descended and eaten everything but the chairs and the napkins.

Dave goes to Lainie Mingenbach's house for a study date. Lainie is Dave's third-favorite girlfriend. She is captain of the pep squad and specializes in doing the cha-cha, the samba, and modern jazz. If it can be danced, she can dance it. This means Dave's first- and second-favorite girlfriends are either sick, grounded, or out babysitting.

Sam and Lucille and I finish watching *The Raven*.

(I don't want to spoil the ending for anybody, but basically everyone in it eventually gets maimed, killed, or arrested.) We learn two more vocab words and do the rest of our homework, and then my dad and I drive Sam and Lucille home in my mom's old pickup truck.

"You know you could be a wonderful swimmer if you put your mind to it, Charlie," my dad tells me when we're finally alone and heading back to our house. "Your grandmother swam like a veritable fish."

"She *was* a fish, Dad." I sigh. "She played championship bridge, too, but that doesn't automatically make me a card player." My parents are always telling me I can do anything. Which is nice, I guess. Only sometimes it just reminds me of how many things I *can't* do.

"I just hate to see you being so afraid, son. That's all. Fear can stop you from doing all sorts of fun and interesting new things."

"But can't fear sometimes be a good thing, Dad? Like fear of putting your hand too near the fire? Or fear of falling off a tall building?"

"Of course, son." Dad smiles as he pulls into our driveway. He shuts off the motor and we go into the house. "We have to learn to tell the difference between our unnecessary childish fears and the fears that keep us safe. That's what growing up is all about."

Balthazar trots up behind us as we quietly climb the stairs. "Sleep well, Charlie. You have a big day tomorrow."

My father pads down the hall and I change into my pj's and get into bed. At least most of me does. The part that's too big to fit sticks out over the end and rests on my brother's old camp trunk. Balthazar curls up next to me. Pretty soon I hear Dave come home and go into the bathroom to brush his teeth. The big spruce tree outside casts an ominous-looking shadow on the ceiling. But then, any shadows you run into after watching *The Raven* are guaranteed to look pretty ominous.

Suddenly a distant shriek pierces the silence of my room. It is the same sound we heard on the way home from the fish store today. I wonder if "fear of shrieks in the night" is an unnecessary childish fear, or a helpful adult one.

Balthazar wakes up and runs to the window, barking his most protective bark. He wouldn't hurt a mouse, but he can sound really ferocious when he thinks something might endanger his family.

Dave shuts off the water. It gets awfully quiet. He tiptoes out of the bathroom and steps on my Buzz Lightyear action figure. "OUCH!!!!!" he screams. Hard molded plastic toys are the worst thing you can possibly step on in your bare feet. "Sorry," Dave whispers.

"It's okay. I'm not asleep." I sit up in my bed and turn on my desk light. Balthazar jumps back into my bed and curls up next to me.

"You'd better get some rest." Dave sits on the edge of his bed and rubs his sore foot. "Don't you have swimming practice tomorrow?"

"How am I supposed to be on the swimming team?" I say. "I don't know how to swim. I don't like to put my head underwater. I'm not even that crazy about drinking the stuff. I'm going to make a complete and total fool of myself."

"Sorry I brought it up," Dave says quietly. He gets under his covers.

"I hate seventh grade. It's like one big opportunity to goof up. Everyone stares at you all the time, just waiting for you to do something stupid so they can talk about it behind your back for the rest of your life."

"Yeah," Dave agrees. "Seventh grade is the pits."

"Amen." I turn off my light.

We both grow quiet. I think about how much I hope they catch the mysterious robber.

Then that horrible sound starts in again. Only this time it's closer. Much closer.

A shiver travels up my body from the tip of my flippers to the top of my pointy head. Balthazar rolls over onto his back and asks for his stomach to be scratched. "What do you think that sound is, Dave?"

"I dunno," he answers. "Maybe a couple of bobcats fighting. Why, what do you think it is?"

"It sounds kind of like a werewolf to me."

Dave chuckles. "You're kidding."

"Not exactly."

"Because there's no such thing as werewolves, okay?" Dave sits up in his bed and looks me right in the eye. "You know that, right?"

"I guess so." I scratch Balthazar carefully on his soft round belly with one of my claws. He's almost asleep again. "You think maybe it's a banshee?"

"No, I do not think it's a banshee." Dave seems pretty adamant. "There's no such thing as banshees, either. You know, for a genius, sometimes you're not very smart."

"Tell me about it."

"You've got to stop watching those scary movies. They're a bad influence on you. Seriously, Charlie. And there's no such thing as vampires. Or zombies. Or the Invisible Man. Or Mothra, for that matter."

"Oh yeah? Well, what about Creatures? Are they imaginary, too?"

For once in his life, my brother can't think of a single thing to say. He just sighs deeply and pulls the covers over his head.

Pretty soon I can't tell who's snoring the loudest: Balthazar or Dave. And I am still awake. I stare up at the ceiling and try to keep my mind off tomorrow's swim practice. Which only makes me think about it more.

If there really was an alternate universe somewhere, I would move there immediately. Just as long as they don't have swimming teams there.

Notes:

Raa!

Raa!

DVR
Alien
tonight

Reminder:
Leave extra
time to walk
Balthazar

Practice **not**
being afraid
of the

water

Hide extra
food in backpack
for when Craig
Dieterly takes
your lunch

I lash
out because
I'm insecure!

6

YOU CAN LEAD A CREATURE TO WATER, BUT YOU CAN'T MAKE HIM SWIM

"WHEN I BLOW my whistle, everybody into the water!" Coach Grubman shouts. Last period just ended and swimming practice is about to start. I am doing my best off to ward off a panic attack. Wish me luck.

Coach Grubman is short and stocky and bald. A large silver whistle hangs from his neck. He looks like one of those people who goes around wrestling alligators on Animal Planet. He ought to feel right at home with me.

"One, two, three. **BRRRRRRING!!!**"

The sound echoes through the pool area, and the fifteen other members of the Stevenson Middle School swimming team leap into the deep end, laughing and screaming and waving their arms.

Not me. I say a silent prayer, hunker down by the gutter, and dip my scaly green legs slowly and carefully

into the shallow end. I have hated going in the water ever since Craig Dieterly pushed my head in the sink and turned on the faucet during first-grade bathroom break. I nearly drowned.

"You there! What do you think you're doing?" Coach Grubman barks.

I was kind of hoping he wouldn't notice me. Not happening.

Coach holds a rubber band in his hands and fiddles with it as he talks. He stretches it. He winds it around his fingers. He balls it up in his fist. "What part of 'everybody into the water' don't you understand, Drinkwater?" He snaps the rubber band like it is an exclamation point.

"Sorry, sir," I reply. "I'm almost in. Just give me a minute here." I teeter at the edge as I lower myself another few millimeters, wishing that Coach Grubman would stop staring at me. The acrid chlorine smell burns my eyes and makes my extremely sensitive nostrils itch. The entire team swims over and gathers around me in the shallow end to watch. The ridiculous brushed satin bathing suit my mother made billows up around my haunches like a giant green parachute.

"What are you wearing, Bigfoot?" Craig Dieterly yells. "You look like the Jolly Green Baby."

"Yeah," says Dirk or Dack Schlissel. "Where'd you get that stupid diaper?"

"Shut up, Schlissel," I reply. "Haven't you ever seen a bathing suit before in your life?"

"Ooh, now it's mad," Craig Dieterly taunts. "I'm so scared." He splashes around and pretends to cry. Everyone thinks it's the funniest thing they have ever seen in their life. "I want my mommy!"

"Can it, Dieterly," Coach Grubman grumbles. "And Drinkwater, you'd better get in the water this instant. I'm starting to lose my patience."

I remain frozen with fear at the edge of the pool,

trying to figure out if fear of going into the shallow end is one of those fear that keeps me safe? Or would that only be fear of going into the deep end?

Coach comes over and unceremoniously dumps me in the rest of the way. I stumble over my tail when it hits the bottom and my head nearly goes under. I inhale a snoutful of water. I cough. I splutter. I try not to panic. The clock on the blue-tiled wall says three o'clock. Only fifty minutes to go.

"Okay, girls," Coach Grubman yells. "Everyone hold on to the edge and kick. It's warm-up time!" I quickly grab on to the side of the pool with my claws and start flapping my flippers.

I've always wondered why the most horrible thing gym teachers can think of to call you is a girl. I don't think girls are so bad. One of my best friends is a girl. My mom's a girl. Or at least she was. Marie Curie was a girl and she discovered radium.

I am just getting used to this kicking thing when Dirk and Dack Schlissel sneak up behind me and pull my bathing suit down. Craig Dieterly starts chanting, "Naked monster on the loose!" and the rest of team whistles and hoots. Grady Hollabird, the only sixth grader on the team, quietly hands me my suit back. I nod gratefully and slip it on as fast as I can.

Coach Grubman blows his whistle again. Everyone freezes as he walks over to the edge of the pool and yells at me, "You're a real troublemaker, you know that, Drinkwater? Five laps. Right now."

"But . . . but . . ." I stammer. This is so unfair. "I didn't *do* anything." Everybody else should be punished. Not me.

"No excuses, Drinkwater," he hollers. "Hop to!"

I keep my head above the water as I inch farther and farther toward the deep end while moving my stumpy little arms around to give the impression that I am doing the breast stroke. Except for everyone making fun of me and feeling like the most uncoordinated idiot in the history of idiots, swimming practice isn't actually as horrible as I thought it would be. It's sort of bearably horrible.

But then Larry Wykoff, the class joker, starts in on me. "Better keep an eye on Drinkwater, Coach. He'll steal the water out of the pool if you're not careful."

"Yeah!" Norm Swerling shouts. "He's one bad Kleptosaur."

I concentrate on Gandhi. And passive resistance.

And getting out of the pool in one piece. I continue my slow walk/swim across the pool.

"Drinkwater's cheating, Coach," one of the Schlissel twins whines. "Don't let him get away with it."

"He's not even putting his head under the water," the other Schlissel adds.

Then Craig Dieterly joins in. "He's just walking around in the pool. Look at him, Coach."

I can remain silent no longer. "Why don't you mind your own beeswax for a change, Dieterly!" I cry.

"Why don't you make me, Gumby?" Craig Dieterly splashes so much water in my face I start to choke. That old familiar suffocating feeling starts in and I have to fight an urge to flee from the pool and hide in the locker room.

"Hey, that's enough, Dieterly!" Coach Grubman shouts. "Go pick on someone your own size."

"Are you kidding?" Craig Dieterly shouts back. "That stinky lizard's *twice* my size!"

"I am not a stinky lizard, I'm a mutant dinosaur, you idiot."

"Can't you two bozos stop fighting for one second?" Coach Grubman sounds really annoyed.

"He started it, Coach," Craig Dieterly complains.

"And I'm ending it." Coach sticks out his arm and points dramatically. "Get to the other end of the pool, Dieterly. Now. There is one captain of this ship and you're talkin' to him." Craig Dieterly reluctantly swims away. "As for you, Drinkwater, four more laps to go. I'm counting."

"It's not fair, Coach Grubman," I complain. "I didn't do anything. I swear."

"I'd call stealing a boatload of Dad's salmon and thirty-two loaves of sourdough bread doing something," Craig Dieterly says angrily. "Wouldn't you, Coach?"

"I didn't steal anything, Coach," I protest. "In this country you are innocent until proven guilty."

"One more peep out of either of you and I'll file a bad behavior report with Principal Muchnick so fast you won't know what hit you," Coach Grubman threatens. "Get your head under the water. Now. Understand?"

"Yes, sir." I stand quietly in the corner of the pool, staring down at the water.

"I don't care if we have to stay here until Christmas, Drinkwater. I am not letting anybody out of this pool until I see that pointy head of yours under the water, and that's final."

I look up at the clock and watch the second hand inching its way around the dial. If I look really closely I can see the minute hand slowly tick off the minutes. I stare at the wall and count the number of chipped tiles and towel hooks. While the rest of the team swims laps, I try to get up the courage to get my snout one inch closer to the surface of the water. "Go ahead," I tell myself. "You can do it. It's only H_2O. Seventy-three percent of the world is covered with the stuff. How bad can it be?"

It's not helping. Every time I try to lower my head it feels like a giant electromagnet is holding it in a viselike grip, and it won't budge.

Coach Grubman paces back and forth. His rubber band is moving around so fast in his hands it's practically a blur. Finally he comes over to me and kneels by the side of the pool.

"What's the matter, kid, didn't anybody ever teach you how to swim?" he whispers gruffly.

"They tried," I reply. "It didn't work."

"You'd think it wouldn't be all that difficult. I mean, what with you having flippers and a tail." Coach puts on his glasses and looks me up and down. "What exactly are you, anyway?"

"I'm a mutant dinosaur, sir." I stare at the surface of

the water, hoping that somehow I will summon up the courage to put my head under it.

"Look, do me a favor." Coach Grubman pulls at his rubber band so hard it looks like it's going to break. "I don't really feel like standing here all day waiting for you to put your damn snout under the water. Try harder, Drinkwater."

"Absolutely. No problem. Here goes . . ." I concentrate with all my might, and tell myself about all the horrible terrible things that will happen to me if I don't listen to Coach Grubman. Then I notice his big silver Timex slip off his wrist and sink into the water like a stone.

Without thinking, I duck my head under the water, whip out my enormous tongue, and grab hold of the watch before it even touches the bottom of the pool. I am handing it back before I realize the seriousness of what I've just done. I'm lucky to be alive. I could easily have hit my head on the bottom of the pool, knocked myself unconscious, and drowned. As it is, I may have breathed water into my lungs and gotten a respiratory infection, which could lead to pneumonia and you *know* how dangerous that can be.

"You're full of surprises, aren't you, kid?" Coach Grubman looks impressed.

"Yes, sir. I hope your watch is okay." I clear my throat and the taste of chlorine in my mouth makes me gag.

"The watch is perfectly fine." He pats his wrist. "It's waterproof. And unbreakable. If it wasn't, I would never have dropped it in the water in the first place." Coach gives me a wink and walks away.

It suddenly dawns on me. "You tricked me, didn't you!"

He turns back. "We coaches have to do whatever it takes to get you meatballs up and running. You call it a trick. I call it standard operating procedure."

"Hmm. So what you're really saying is that the end justifies the means. An interesting point of view. I'm not sure I agree with you. But . . . it's a topic worth further exploration. Perhaps we could continue this discussion on dry land, if you catch my drift."

Coach Grubman kneels down and speaks to me simply and quietly. "You talk too much, Drinkwater. Why don't you tell that mighty mouth of yours to shut up every once in a while and start trusting your darn instincts. A fish doesn't have to go to school to learn how to be a fish. It just knows. Now get out of here." He tosses me a towel. I catch it in my claws and wipe the water from my eyes.

Coach puts his megaphone up to his mouth and

shouts at the Sardines. "Everybody out of the pool!" Fifteen exhausted swimmers slowly emerge from the water, grab their towels, and shuffle to the locker room. "Remember: it's the Stevenson Sardines versus the Carbondale Catfish in only three more days. Eat right. Stay fit. See you at Thursday's practice!"

I clutch the edge of the pool with my claws and start dragging my massive torso out of the shallow end. Coach Grubman comes over, grabs me by the shoulders, and helps me to my feet. I mean flippers.

"So do you think you could just tell Principal Muchnick I'm a hopeless case and kick me off the team and save us all a lot of grief?"

"Not on your life. Something tells me there's a swimmer lurking somewhere deep inside of you, Drinkwater. I'm not done with you yet." Coach Grubman snaps his rubber band, turns on his heels, and is gone before you can say "sometimes your day turns out to be just as awful as you thought it was going to be."

7
THINGS THAT GO BUMP IN THE NIGHT

"SO WHAT'S IT like being on the swimming team?" Sam asks. After changing out of my swimsuit, I've just met up with Sam and Lucille next to the band shell in Ogilvie Park. "Did it live up to all your expectations?"

"Hmm . . . let's see," I begin. "I was humiliated beyond my wildest dreams, I swallowed so much water I wanted to throw up, and Craig Dieterly poked me so hard in the chest he nearly gave me a subdural hematoma. A perfect ending to a perfect day."

"I'm jealous," Sam replies.

"Hey, do you think you guys could walk and be sarcastic at the same time?" Lucille seems frustrated. "In case you forgot, we're on a mission."

"Oh yeah. Sure," I answer. And we are off.

We head over to 63 Maple Drive, Aunt Harriet and Uncle Marvin's house. Of the three recent victims, my uncle's the only one who was actually present during his crime. We are hoping he will be able to shed some light on the perp.

So far the police haven't come up with any leads. But we are determined to solve the Great Decatur Robbery Mystery and prove I didn't do anything once and for all. Hopefully before Thursday's swimming practice.

I cock my pointy head to one side, prick up my earflaps, and listen for the unusual wailing sound we heard yesterday. But all I can hear is the wind blowing the leaves around and a flock of noisy starlings circling overhead.

"Junior Scientists of America, put on your thinking caps," Sam announces. He looks at us to make sure we are paying our utmost attention. "For every crime, there is a perpetrator. For every perpetrator, there is a motive. It's Criminology 101." I can practically hear the wheels turning in Sam's head. "Let's pretend you're the perp, Lucille. What would make you steal a bag of dirty old shoes? Name your motive."

"Injustice?" Lucille says tentatively. "Maybe the shoes were mine to begin with."

"And?"

"Maybe Charlie's uncle stole them from me, and I was just stealing them back." Lucille bites her lip. "It could have happened."

"Okay," Sam replies. "Let's say it did. Then why did you steal Mr. Dieterly's salmon and all that sourdough bread from the cafeteria?"

"Hmmm." Lucille scratches her head. "Good question. Why would the person who stole a bag of shoes also want to steal all that salmon? And then break into the cafeteria and take thirty-two loaves of sourdough bread?"

"Maybe he wasn't after the shoes, Sam," I suggest. "Maybe the perp thought there was something valuable hidden inside of the bag."

"Like what? Money?" Lucille asks.

"I was thinking more along the lines of stock certificates. Or maybe a deed to a house or something," I reply.

"Exactly!" Lucille says eagerly. "The kind of thing

you might actually hide in an old shoe and then forget about."

"Now you're cooking," Sam says. "If we can figure out a motive for the O'Connor robbery, it'll be a lot easier to narrow down our search for suspects."

"Oh no," I whisper, terrified. "Don't move."

"What is it, Charlie?" Lucille asks. "Are you okay?"

"No." I point to a clump of leaves near my flipper. "Look."

"It's just a roach," Sam says. "What's the big deal?"

"It's a giant water beetle. They have giant wings and fly in your face, and if I don't get out of here immediately I am going to pass out." I start running. Sam and Lucille follow close behind. Fear number two thousand and six: insects that *look* like they could sting you.

"Is it following us?" I ask, too scared to look back.

"I don't think so," Lucille answers. "Giant water beetles generally don't follow people. They're sort of more into not getting stepped on."

"Thank God." I slow down and try to catch my breath. "It almost touched me."

"Look," Sam announces. "We're here. 63 Maple Drive."

"Propelled by fear," Lucille jokes. "Fastest way to travel."

I ring the bell with my claw, and we wait for someone to answer the door. The house is small but tidy. The lawn is in good shape, and the shutters are painted a crisp, bright green. From the looks of the place you would have no idea that my aunt and uncle are two of strangest individuals you have ever come across.

Uncle Marvin opens the door a crack and peers out at us. He has a long white mustache that droops over the corners of his mouth like a walrus, and a mop of unruly gray hair that looks like animals are living in it. He wears a ratty bathrobe over ancient striped yellow and blue pajamas, even though it is four thirty in the afternoon.

"Hi, Uncle Marvin." I step onto the porch and hold out my claw. Instead of shaking it, my uncle just stands there looking quizzically at me. His mouth hangs open. It always does. That's why everyone in my family refers to him as "Marvin the Mouth Breather."

"Does your uncle's mouth always hang down like that?" Lucille whispers.

"Only when he breathes," I reply.

"Who is it, Marv?" Aunt Harriet's booming voice rumbles through the house like distant thunder.

"It's your mutant dinosaur nephew and some of his pals," Uncle Marvin calls back. "He's even bigger than I remembered. Come have a look-see." Uncle Marvin sneezes so loudly it hurts my earflaps.

"We were wondering if you would mind answering a few questions, Mr. O'Connor—" Sam begins.

Before Uncle Marvin has a chance to reply, Aunt Harriet appears behind him in the doorway. A short, round woman with a beak-like nose and tiny black eyes, she says, "If you kids came over to wish me happy birthday, you're three days early."

"We just stopped by to ask a few questions, Aunt Harriet."

"My, oh my!" my aunt exclaims. "Look at you, Charlie. You're getting greener and slimier every day."

Sam and Lucille shoot me quick "what's up with your weird aunt?" looks.

"Yeah," Uncle Marvin says unenthusiastically. "He sure is." He sneezes again. Harriet hands him a Kleenex.

"Did anybody ever tell you that you look just like your grandmother Nana Wallabird, may she rest in peace?" Aunt Harriet shuffles onto the porch to get a closer look at me. "Same eyes. Same sloping forehead. And just look at that tail." She shakes her head approvingly. "He's a Wallabird all right, isn't he, Marv?"

"You took the words right out of my mouth," Uncle Marvin replies.

"Well, don't just stand there, Charlie," Aunt Harriet orders. "Hug your old auntie." She opens her arms and throws them around me, squeezing me so tightly I can hardly catch my breath.

"Great to see you too, Aunt Harriet." I gasp for air as I disentangle myself from her grasp.

"Say, I remember you kids!" Aunt Harriet eyes Sam and Lucille. "You must be . . . Lucille. And of course you're Sam. I could never forget that fake nose ring! Come on in, everybody. I'll get you a nice hot cup of lemon verbena."

"I'm afraid we can't stay very long, Aunt Harriet." I step back on the little porch. It sags under my enormous weight. "We just wanted to ask a few questions about Uncle Marvin's robbery, if that's okay."

"Be my guest." Aunt Harriet cocks her head to one side and listens attentively.

"Can you describe the person who stole your bag of shoes, Mr. O'Connor?" Lucille asks.

"Like I told the police, whoever took those things went to great pains to avoid being seen. I didn't even catch a glimpse of the guy."

"Are you absolutely sure of that, sir?" Lucille asks.

"As sure as I'm standing here," my uncle answers.

"Marv always tells the truth, Lucille," my aunt says. "You can depend on Marv O'Connor like you can depend on it to rain on your new shoes. If you have any." She points at my bare flippers and chuckles.

"Can you describe the exact circumstances of the robbery, Mr. O'Connor?" Sam asks.

"Why make such a big fuss about a bunch of old shoes?" Aunt Harriet puts her hands on her stout hips. "Now if someone stole my false teeth, *that* would be worth talking about."

"It may seem unnecessary, Mrs. O'Connor," Lucille explains. "But sometimes even the most mundane detail can provide a critical link in breaking a difficult case."

"Well, when you put it that way . . ." Uncle Marvin begins. "It happened yesterday morning. Seven twenty-five a.m., to be precise. I know that because I'd just finished watching the morning news with that Joe Jefferson guy who looks like his face is made out of wax. I'd cleaned out my closet and was planning to bring my entire collection of rare shoes over to my insurance company for an appraisal. I stuffed them into a garbage bag, changed out of my slippers, and put on my coat. The brown twill with the shiny leather buttons. Got it for my thirty-seventh birthday. . . . You know that coat, Harriet?"

"How could I forget, Marv, sweetie?" Aunt Harriet sighs. "I gave it to you."

"That's right! Ahh . . . ahh . . . ahh . . . *choo!!!*" Uncle Marvin holds out his hand. Aunt Harriet puts another Kleenex into it. "Thanks, hon."

"Excuse me, guys," I interrupt. "Was there anything out of the ordinary about those shoes?"

"There certainly was, Charlie!" Uncle Marvin exclaims. "I had some extremely unusual specimens in there, including a pair of size eleven Gucci loafers that Donald Trump wore to his daughter's wedding. They had some actual wedding cake stuck to the heel. They were real beauts. Every shoe has a story to tell if you listen carefully enough."

"Wow. That's really . . . um . . . interesting, Mr.

O'Connor," Sam says. "Anyway. Did you maybe leave anything inside any of them?"

"Yeah," Lucille adds. "Like a significant letter . . . or maybe a deed to a building? Or a stock certificate?"

"Nope." Uncle Marvin shakes his head.

Lucille sighs. "Anything else either of you remembers about what happened? Think hard."

Uncle Marvin scrunches up his forehead and shuts his eyes. "I remember taking those shoes out of my closet like it was yesterday."

"It *was* yesterday, Marv," Aunt Harriet whispers.

Uncle Marvin continues, undeterred. "I happen to know there was nothing inside any of those shoes because Harriet made me shake each one out to make sure I hadn't dropped any loose change in any of them. She just loves loose change. She collects it. Don't you, Harriet?"

"I collect coins of all nations that begin with the letter *B*," Aunt Harriet answers proudly. "I'd love to show you kids sometime." I told you my aunt was eccentric. "The Bulgarian stotinka is one of my favorites. A hundred stotinki make up one lev. I'll run in and bring you each a couple for a special treat. They're a darling little coin."

"Maybe later, Aunt Harriet," I say. "Isn't there anything else you remember?"

"Nope. Nothing in that garbage bag except old shoes. I'd swear on a stack of Bibles," Uncle Marvin says. "I would bet my life on it. I have been training my mind to remember the slightest details for years, using the Silva Mind Control Method. Even an idiot can tune out the static of everyday challenges and . . . and . . . wait a minute."

Uncle Marvin's mouth droops open a little farther, which is pretty amazing and actually sort of disturbing when you think about it. "There *was* something else in that bag. Why didn't I think of that before? I took out the garbage along with the shoes, only I was in a hurry because it looked like it was going to snow and I'm just getting over a bad cold, so I tucked the garbage inside the bag of shoes and forgot all about it. That robber didn't just make off with my rare used shoe collection, he got a jumbo portion of last night's leftovers as well." Uncle Marvin sneezes several times loudly.

"So much for that stack of Bibles. Let's put you to bed, honey. You're not ready for company."

"Do you remember what was in those leftovers?" I ask.

"I sure do," my uncle replies, sniffling loudly. "Succotash, half of a baked potato, and a perfectly good noodle pudding. I dropped it on the floor and your aunt made me throw it away."

"I certainly did," Aunt Harriet says. "Who in their right mind would eat a noodle pudding after it fell on the floor?"

"Me," Uncle Marvin says simply.

"Thanks a lot, Mr. and Mrs. O'Connor," Sam says. "That was really helpful." We turn to leave.

"There's one more thing," Uncle Marvin adds. We freeze in our tracks. "Whoever took those things smelled kind of funny."

"What did he smell like, Uncle Marvin?" I ask. "It's very important."

"He smelled . . . sort of . . . sort of like . . . he smelled like old seaweed and rotting fish."

"We'd better be on our way now, Mr. and Mrs. O'Connor," Lucille says abruptly. She gives me an anxious look.

"Come back soon, Charlie," Aunt Harriet says. "Don't be a stranger!" She grabs me and hugs me a little too tightly.

Lucille and Sam take my arms and practically drag

me off the porch. We race down the road. We are halfway to my house by the time Sam finally speaks. "Are
you absolutely sure you don't have an identical twin in an
alternate reality, Charlie? It would explain everything."

"At this point I'm not absolutely sure of anything." I
sniff my stumpy little arm. Old seaweed and rotting fish
all right. The description fits me like a glove.

But it wasn't me. It couldn't have been. WHAT IS
GOING ON HERE?????

"Okay. What do we know?" Lucille says. "Charlie,
you start."

"Three crimes, one motive: hunger."

"I'll buy it," Sam agrees.

"Do we all go with the one-perp theory?" Lucille
asks.

"I sure do," Sam answers. "How about a description?"

"About my height. Claws instead of hands. Smells
like me." I stare down at my big webbed feet. "Looks like
me. But not me."

"It would be so easy if it were, Charlie," Lucille adds.

"But it's not," Sam says firmly. "The same uh . . .
creature . . . cannot occupy two different spaces at the
same time."

I am so busy trying on various crime scenarios I don't open my big jaws to speak until we reach the corner of Lonesome Lane and Cedar Street and I am almost home. As the last ray of sunlight disappears behind a row of distant beech trees I am the first to break the silence. "There's probably an obvious answer just staring us in the face. We are so going to kick ourselves when we finally figure out who this guy is." I stomp my flippers on the icy sidewalk to get my circulation going.

"Yeah," Lucille says quietly. "I sure hope so."

Sam blows on his fingers to warm them up. "I have a piano recital this weekend and I promised my mom I'd practice today. I better get going."

"Oops, I almost forgot. I'm taking my ferrets to the vet for their shots," Lucille says. "I've got to run."

"Fine," I say, "but don't forget: we have an emergency meeting of the Junior Scientists of America tonight. My house. Six o'clock sharp."

My friends nod their agreement, and then they take off. And I am alone.

I don't think we're ever going to solve this mystery. No wonder everybody keeps thinking I did it. If I wasn't me, I'd think I did it, too. Who else could it be? I can do the crossword puzzle in the Sunday *New York Times* in pen without even thinking. You'd think I could solve a little thing like a mystery.

It's getting dark. A full moon is just beginning its ascent, and I can feel the temperature dropping as the wind picks up. I've got to get home before nightfall or I'll be in real trouble.

I can just make out my house in the distance when that terrifying wailing sound starts again. I pick up speed.

No need to panic, I tell myself. It's just those pesky raccoons again. *Keep moving, Charlie. You're almost home.*

I break into a trot. I try not to think about the fact that there is a horrible monster following me and concentrate instead on the sudden increase in the raccoon population due to last winter's favorable weather conditions. *Faster, Charlie. Faster.*

All of a sudden the noise stops and everything grows frighteningly quiet. All I can hear is the sound of my own labored breathing as I break into a gallop. I barely manage to avoid tripping over the roots of the giant oak that welcomes me back to my block. Never have I been so happy to see a tree.

Okay. You're almost there, Charlie. Home. I can practically smell the roast beef browning in the oven. In another minute I'll be sneaking Balthazar roast potatoes under the table and trying to explain to my mother why I got home so late.

And then I notice the massive, hulking being lurking behind the pine trees directly ahead of me. I come to a dead halt. Too terrified to utter a sound. Too frightened to move.

It's so dark that I can't get a good look at the thing. I can just make out a pair of evil-looking, almond-shaped eyes peering out from behind the tree, glinting at me in the dim light of the rising moon. The thing's massive

jaws hang open, revealing row after row of razor-sharp fangs. Its raspy breath comes in fits and starts. I feel like somebody has just picked me up and dropped me into the middle of my own worst nightmare.

"Noooooo!!!" The involuntary scream escapes from my lips, and I run for my life.

The thing follows after me, crashing noisily through piles of leaves and fallen branches. I take a quick look back as it trips over its enormous tail and goes tumbling headfirst into a streetlight. It crashes to the ground like a giant tree, landing in a crumpled, motionless heap. It doesn't appear to be breathing. Blood oozes from a nasty gash on the side of its scaly green head.

Is the thing dead or just stunned? I stand frozen in my tracks, gasping for air, not knowing what to do. Finally my curiosity gets the better of me and I make my way cautiously through the misty darkness to get a better look at the fallen creature.

The light from the lamppost above casts its eerie glow onto the thing's head. I can tell in one shiver-inducing instant that the motionless being on the ground is a mirror image of myself. Same massive jaws. Same earflaps. Same flippers. The mystery is a mystery no more.

I am not the only one of my kind.

8

ONE GOOD CREATURE DESERVES ANOTHER

"THAT'S INCREDIBLE!" Sam's eyes bug out and his purple hair looks like it is standing on end. "Are you sure?"

"Of course I'm sure," I say indignantly. "Scales, claws, a tail—the whole nine yards. The thing is *exactly* like me, except a million times more ferocious."

"Charlie, a million times zero is still zero," Lucille says.

"Let me put it this way, guys: the thing makes Godzilla look like a gerbil. Okay?"

It's now almost six p.m. and Sam, Lucille, and I are

sitting in my den, pretending to watch *Invasion of the Body Snatchers* for the three millionth time while we hold our emergency meeting of the Junior Scientists of America. Kevin McCarthy is running for his life as a mob of angry aliens chases him through a dark and winding tunnel. We're not paying attention. We have bigger fish to fry. Much bigger.

"Your clone is the robber," Lucille announces. "I'd bet my life on it."

"Double ditto," Sam says happily. "This explains everything!"

"Yeah," I reply. "Except who that other creature is."

"And what he's doing here," Lucille adds.

"And where he came from," I say. "Other than that, it explains everything."

"So what do we do now?" I ask.

"Simple, big guy," Sam explains. "We apprehend the *other* creature and turn him in to the police, you get your Get Out of Jail Free card, Muchnick takes you off the swim team, everyone knows you're innocent, and things go back to normal."

"Define *normal*." I wave my tail in the air.

"I still think you should tell your mother, Charlie," Lucille insists.

"I don't," I reply. "If I told my mom there was a dangerous monster on the loose, she wouldn't let me out of her sight for a second, and we'd *never* be able to capture the creature."

"True." Sam picks at the peeling black polish on his fingernails. "And who knows if she'd believe him anyway? An identical twin monster running around getting Charlie into trouble? Even *you* had trouble believing it, Lucille, and you heard the monster with your own two ears. I'm with the big guy." He nods at me.

"Then you should talk to Mr. Arkady, Charlie," Lucille suggests. "He's always telling us to come to him with our problems."

"But what could he do to help?" I wonder.

"You never know until you ask," Lucille answers.

"I'm home!" My dad slams the front door. Balthazar barks and runs into the hallway to greet him.

"Dinner's ready," Mom calls from the kitchen. "Come and get it!"

I turn off the TV. "How do you suggest we go about catching this thing?"

"We set a trap," Lucille suggests.

"Just what I was thinking, Lucille," Sam says. "All we need is the right bait." They both look at me.

"Uh-uh. No way. I may be big and green and scaly, but I'm not crazy. I'm not going out there looking for trouble. That creature could tear me in half in two seconds without even breaking a sweat."

"Lizards don't sweat, Charlie," Lucille explains. "It's a commonly known fact. In hot weather the frilled dragon has been known to compensate by running around on its hind legs, thus generating a cool breeze and lowering its body temperature."

"That's very reassuring, Lucille," I reply.

My dad pokes his head into the den. "Hurry up, kids. I'm so hungry I could eat a table and have enough room left over for some chairs." There's no arguing with a starving father.

We go wash our hands and claws and then everyone runs to take their place at the dining room table, except Dave, who is still at football practice. Big surprise.

"Please pass the potatoes, Mrs. D." Sam places his napkin in his lap.

As my mom hands Sam the platter, my dad lugs in the little TV from the kitchen. "Get that thing out of here, honey," Mom complains. "Dinner is a time for relaxing and communicating."

My dad puts the TV on the buffet next to the dining

room table. "You're not going to believe what Al Swanson just texted me." Al works in direct sales at Balls in Malls, the sporting goods store my dad manages. "Everybody's talking about it." Dad turns the TV on, and Joe Jefferson appears, as tan and perfect as ever.

"You're impossible, Fred Drinkwater," my mom snorts as she heads for the kitchen.

"Quiet, honey. Listen to this," Dad urges.

"This late-breaking news just in, folks: the mysterious Decatur robber strikes again. This time the innocent victim is the proprietor of a successful chain of specialty food shops called Beautiful Bites. Tell us, Mr. Hollabird, in your own words, exactly what happened?"

"What?!" Mom exclaims. "Mr. Hollabird? That's awful." She rushes back to the dining room, sets the roast beef on the table, and plants herself in front of the television set. "Can you believe this, Fred? I sure hope he's okay."

"Shh, Doris. I want to hear what he has to say."

Lucille and Sam and I get up from our seats and gather around the little set.

". . . the thief was gone by the time we got there, Joe." Mr. Hollabird wipes the perspiration from his forehead with his sleeve. "He made a terrible mess of one of my kiosks. Ripped the counter right off the wall with his bare hands. Nearly tore down the door. On top of that, he stole three cases of my freshly baked sugar-free cherry pies and a box of my low-fat soy cheese croissants."

"Low-fat soy cheese croissants!" my mom exclaims. "Now why didn't I think of that?"

"Please, Doris!" My dad turns up the volume.

"Any idea who did it, Mr. Hollabird?" Joe Jefferson asks.

"Beats me. All I know is that it must have been one tall thief."

"Why do you say that?"

"Those cherry pies were stored on top of a twelve-foot cabinet, Joe. And whoever stole them didn't use a ladder."

"My, oh my." Joe Jefferson shakes his head. "We'll return with tomorrow's weather after this important word from our . . ." My dad flicks off the set.

One tall thief. Great. At this point not only will I be on the dreaded swimming team for eternity, I will probably have to join the football team as well.

"They'd better catch that guy before he hurts somebody, that's all I can say." My dad gets up from the table and puts the TV back in the kitchen.

"I didn't do it," I say quietly. "I know it looks like I did. But I didn't."

"We were with him all afternoon, Mrs. Drinkwater," Lucille says earnestly. "He couldn't have done it."

"Even if he had wanted to," Sam adds.

"We know you didn't, Charlie." My mom takes my claw and holds it firmly and carefully in her hands. "Your father and I trust you completely."

My dad returns to the table and puts his napkin in his lap. "You may have transformed on the outside, but on the inside you're still the same Charlie Drinkwater you always were. And Charlie Drinkwater doesn't go around stealing and lying. Period. End of discussion."

It's sure great to have parents who believe in you. Especially when almost no one else does.

When the phone rings in the kitchen a moment later, we all ignore it. It's a family rule: no texting, no reading e-mails, and no answering the phone at the dinner table. But after several annoying minutes it's apparent that whoever's calling just won't give up.

Finally Mom can't take it any longer. "Oh, for heaven's sake," she complains as she gets up and goes into the kitchen.

I strain my earflaps to hear what she is saying, but even with my powerful hearing all I can make out is some mumbling.

After a minute my mom comes back to the table looking extremely confused. She slowly sits back down and puts her napkin in her lap.

"What happened, Mom?" I ask.

"That was Mr. Hollabird," she begins.

"Does he love your recipes?" I ask, excited.

"Are you a hit, Mrs. D?" Sam asks.

"I'm afraid not, kids." My mom reaches over and puts her hand gently on the side of my gaping jaws. "Now Charlie, I don't want you to be upset. Mr. Hollabird is convinced you robbed his store."

"What?" my father gasps. "That's ridiculous. Charlie would never do a thing like that." Sam and Lucille nod their heads supportively.

"That is exactly what I told Mr. Hollabird. I said he was jumping to conclusions, and when all the evidence was in, he would see how wrong he was. I gave him every opportunity to apologize."

"What did he say, Mom?" I ask.

"He said if you confess he'll go easy on you. But if you don't . . . he's going to bar me from the baking competition."

My fork slips from my claw and hits my plate with a loud clanging sound. I cannot believe my earflaps.

"Can you imagine?" Mom goes on. "The nerve of that man. I gave him a piece of my mind, believe you me."

"I'll confess, Mom." I rise up suddenly from my seat at the table, forget to duck, and hit my head on the ceiling. A light sprinkling of plaster dust lands on the quesadillas. "I can't let that man punish you for something I didn't even do. It's not fair. You've worked all your life to perfect those recipes."

"That's so sweet, Charlie, but I could never let you do that," my mom says vehemently. "I wouldn't *consider* working for that man now. Not after what he said about you. Not even if he got on his hands and knees and begged me to forgive him."

I sit back down. Mom wets her napkin in her water glass and wipes the top of my head.

"But Mom," I begin. "This is your big break!"

"I already have everything I need, sweetie. I have my

family and my health and a wonderful career. There will be plenty of other opportunities."

"Your mother's right," my dad adds. "Let's finish our dinner and get on with our lives. Mr. Hollabird will just have to find some other nutritionally oriented talented dessert chef to take your mother's place."

We all continue eating as if nothing happened. Vegetables are passed. The table is cleared. We dig into my mom's delicious flourless chocolate soufflé. But I can think of only one thing: I must capture the creature and bring it to justice. I will find a way. This isn't just about *me* anymore. It's about something much bigger than that. It's about my family. And I would do anything for them. Anything.

9
BAIT AND SWITCH

"SO WHAT DO WE do now?" Sam asks. He paces around my room, anxiously drumming his fingers on his substantial belly. Mom and Dad are still doing the dinner dishes while my friends and I are supposedly finishing our homework. As if.

"Call the police?" Lucille sits on the edge of Dave's bed, tying and retying her size twelve saddle shoes. To say Lucille's feet are big is like saying water is wet.

"What good would that do?" Sam counters. "They've been on the case for the last thirty-six hours and as far as

I can tell they haven't come up with a single lead. At least Charlie's actually laid eyes on the thing."

"True," I say quietly. "I hate to admit it, but we'll just have to catch the creature ourselves and do our best not to get killed."

"That would be nice." Lucille looks up. "I would really prefer to avoid death by homicidal maniac."

"So how exactly do you plan to do that, Charlie?" Sam asks.

"You know that old dry well behind the fairgrounds?"

"Sure," Lucille says. "It's all boarded up. Nobody ever goes there anymore."

"What are you driving at, Drinkwater?" Sam asks.

"We uncover it, disguise it with leaves and branches, lure the creature over to it with some kind of bait, like maybe . . . um . . ."

"Fish!" Lucille exclaims. "We know he loves fish because he just stole all that salmon from Mr. Dieterly's store."

"I'm loving it," Sam says. "The creature falls in, the authorities come and arrest him, and you're not a suspect anymore, Charlie."

"And I won't have to be on the swimming team anymore," I say happily. "Or get expelled. And Mr. Hollabird will ask my mom to sell her desserts to Beautiful Bites. Happy ending all around!"

"This whole thing sounds incredibly familiar." Lucille scratches her head. "Didn't we see something like this once in a movie?

"We sure did," Sam says. "That's how Jack Driscoll and Carl Denham, fearless explorers, trapped the mighty King Kong. We watched the movie in fifth grade. I had nightmares for a week."

"What are we waiting for?" I grab my backpack and head downstairs. Sam and Lucille follow close behind.

"What's the plan?" Lucille asks.

"We're going to my house to finish our English report. It's due Friday," Sam whispers. "Follow my lead."

"What do we do when they insist on driving us to your house, Sam?" Lucille asks. "Because they will and you know it."

"We let them," Sam says.

"No," I say firmly. "We *ask* them to drive us before they bring it up. It's much less likely to raise their suspicions."

"Bingo," Sam says. "And *then* we go trap us a creature."

My parents are in the den playing gin rummy for pennies. They have kept a running total for the last twenty years. So far my dad owes my mom over seven thousand dollars. My mom says she's willing to compromise. She'll accept a used Volkswagen convertible instead of the money.

"We have to go to Sam's to finish our English report, Mom and Dad. All our notes are on his computer and it's due Friday. Can you drive us?"

"We'd be happy to, Charlie." Mom gathers up the cards and puts the box into the drawer. "I'm glad you asked. With that robber lurking around out there you can't be too careful."

My dad carefully counts up the score. "I owe you another two dollars and fifty cents, Doris."

"Put it on my tab, Fred." She gets up from the table. "Wear your gloves, kids. It's cold out."

I sneak the leftover salmon from tonight's dinner out of the fridge and into my backpack while my mom and my dad put on their overcoats. Then we all pile into my mom's beat-up red pickup truck and head for Sam's.

"How long do you think you'll be, kids?" my dad asks as we chug down Lonesome Lane

"I'd say an hour and a half, Mr. D," Sam replies. "It's a pretty complicated project."

"What's it about?" my mom asks.

"The use of the subjunctive tense in the short stories of Edgar Allan Poe."

I don't know how Sam comes up with this stuff so quickly. For a basically honorable guy, he lies like a rug.

"That's very interesting, Sam," my mom comments. "Can you give me an example?"

"I'm afraid I can't, Mrs. D," Sam replies without batting an eyelash. "Many of Poe's short stories are no longer in print. That's why it's taking us so long to write our report. Finding the original source material is a real back-breaker."

If they ever make lying an Olympic sport, Sam's a gold-medal winner for sure.

"We'll be back to pick you up at eight forty-five on the dot, Charlie," my mom announces as we pull into Sam's driveway and hop out of the truck. "Please be ready to go then."

Sam, Lucille, and I wave good-bye before going into

Sam's house. My mom and dad wait out front until they see the front door close behind us. I love my parents, but sometimes they're harder to shake than burrs off a woolen mitten.

"We have to hunt fast. We don't have much time," Sam says. "We've got to be back here by the time your folks come to get you, Charlie. No matter what."

We head straight for the living room, where Mrs. Endervelt sits in front of the big TV, watching the local news. She looks up briefly. "Hi, kids. What's up?" Sam's mom is a no-nonsense, practical type of mom. Wire-framed glasses. Gray hair. Keds.

Joe Jefferson's phony deep voice booms out over the speaker. "The mysterious Decatur robber is still on the loose, ladies and gentlemen. If you see anything suspicious, call our crime-stoppers hotline. That's 555-6600."

"We have to go to Lucille's house to work on our English project, Mom. We forgot we left our notes there."

"That's nice, Sam," Mrs. Endervelt answers. Not one question. Not a "does Lucille's mom know you're coming?" Or a "what time will you be back?" Or a "did you finish your homework?" Nothing.

If any other kid in middle school dyed his hair purple, painted his fingernails black, and wore a fake nose ring, his mom would probably chain him to his desk and throw away the key. Not Sue Endervelt.

"Help yourselves to whatever's in the fridge before you go, kids. Just be sure to leave something for your dad, Sam. He's coming home late tonight and he'll be starving." Mr. Endervelt works at a recycling plant. He looks just like Sam. Only taller. And he doesn't do Goth.

"Thanks, Mrs. Endervelt!" I call, and we quickly raid the fridge

"Let's get out of here," Lucille whispers. We dump our creature bait into a plastic bag and head for the door.

"Don't work too hard, kids," Mrs. Endervelt calls.

"Don't worry, we won't!" I shout.

We beeline across the front lawn and head for the corner of Lonesome Lane and Cedar Street, the site of my previous encounter. The street is deserted. The fog is as thick as cotton. A damp penetrating chill rises up from the sidewalk. I can barely see two feet in front of me.

"Tonight reminds of that scene in *The Wolf Man*," Sam says quietly. "Where Larry Talbot rescues his friend and gets bitten by the Wolf Man and turns into a wolf. Good thing it's not a full moon. Or is it?" Sam looks up at the sky. "It's pretty hard to tell with all that fog and mist."

"Must you say every single terrifying thought that enters your brain, Sam Endervelt?" Lucille sighs.

"Quiet. I smell creature." I twist my long thick neck around and breathe in the frosty air. "It's not far away. It must have smelled the bait and come out to feed."

"What do we do now?" Sam asks nervously.

"We keep it interested." I take a hunk of salmon from my book bag and start shredding it into bite-sized pieces with my claws.

"Whatever you're doing smells like you've got an entire school of dead fish in there." Lucille looks like she is about to throw up.

"That's the point, Lucille. Now you guys run ahead and cover up that old well while I lure the creature over to it." It's less than a mile to the fairgrounds. Even taking into account Sam's legendary slowness, they should be there in less than fifteen minutes. I take another deep breath. "Hurry. He's getting closer."

"Take your time, pal," Sam warns. "We don't want you and Mr. Creature arriving before we're ready for our guest."

"Get going," I urge. "Before it's too late!"

"Are you sure you'll be okay by yourself, Charlie?" Lucille hesitates.

"Sure I'm sure." I try to sound confident. I'm not. "Get out of here. I'm not kidding."

Sam and Lucille hurry off at last to prepare the trap, and I am left alone in the murky darkness. Except for the rustling of the wind through the big old pines that line the street, all is quiet. I scatter bits of salmon behind me as I walk.

Suddenly a twig snaps. And then another one.

My earflaps perk up. I detect distant footsteps. It sounds like they're heading toward me. I walk faster. So does whatever is following me. The smell of mutant dinosaur is so strong it makes my nostrils tingle.

A chill runs down my long, spiky neck. I am wrestling with two of my biggest fears at once: fear of the dark, and fear of monsters. The fact that this monster looks exactly like me doesn't seem to make me any less afraid. If anything, it's scarier. Because it's stranger.

The more bait I drop, the closer the footsteps get, until finally the creature is so close I can hear it snarling and grunting as it tears into the salmon with its massive fangs.

And then all of a sudden the sound stops and everything is quiet. I don't know whether to keep walking and risk losing the creature, or to stop and risk getting attacked.

I am shaking like a leaf. And it's not because of the icy chill in the air. Nope. It's just plain old abject fear that is turning my legs into a mass of quivering Jell-O.

I wonder if Sam and Lucille have got the trap prepared yet. I wonder if the creature has lost interest and sought refuge in the neighboring woods. Or is it lying low and planning to take me by surprise? I decide to move on and see if that rouses the creature.

Which is when a voice in the dark calls to me, stopping me in my tracks. "Please don't leave. I need talk to you. Please." It is a gentle, human voice.

The clouds break and a silvery shaft of moonlight illuminates the scaly green mutant dinosaur standing across the road, staring right at me. It makes its way slowly toward me.

"I won't hurt you, Charlie. I'm so glad I found you. I'm your cousin, Stanley. I've been looking for you everywhere."

10
STRANGERS IN THE NIGHT

"WHERE HAVE YOU been, pal?" Sam asks when I finally arrive at the fairgrounds alone. "We thought you were dead. Do you have any idea how hard it was to cover up this abandoned well?" He points to the tangle of leaves and branches he and Lucille have cleverly arranged.

"Where's the creature?" Lucille looks around. "I thought it was following you."

"Not anymore," I reply.

"What do you mean?" Sam pulls on his nose ring so hard I am afraid he may pull off his nose. "You were supposed to lure him into the trap, pal."

"That was before."

"Before what?" Lucille asks. "C'mon. Tell."

"I can't. We have to take the Mainframe pledge first. That's how ultrasecret and important this is." My friends and I raise our right hands (in my case my right claw) and recite in unison:

"Our lips are sealed.
Our eyes are shut.
We promise not to reveal
The secret which goes to our graves with us.
This truth we forever conceal."

Then we jump in the air, turn around three times, clap our hands, and shout, "Eternity sucks!" I get so dizzy I stumble over my tail and nearly fall on Sam.

"So tell us the secret already," Sam says breathlessly. "I'm exhausted from taking the pledge."

"Well, first of all, he's incredibly nice. He's more than nice. He's amazing. He's brave and thoughtful and . . ."

"Slow down." Lucille waves her long skinny arms around. "Let me get this straight. HE'S NICE??? I thought he was terrifying and dangerous."

"Not when you get to know him," I reply. "He even

wants to teach me how to swim. Can you believe it? Not that I'm exactly *dying* to learn how or anything. But it was nice of him to offer."

"How did swimming even come up as a topic of discussion?" Sam asks.

"We were telling each other stuff about our lives," I explain. "And I mentioned how much I hate being on the swimming team. Being a non-swimmer and all. And guess what he told me? He's my cousin! Can you believe it?"

"That is beyond amazing, Charlie!" Lucille gasps.

"I know. He's Aunt Harriet and Uncle Marvin's kid. He said he turned into a creature just like me when he was twelve years old. He left Decatur nine years ago to go live under Crater Lake with the rest of our long-lost relatives. Evidently everyone was so sad he was gone they couldn't bear to talk about him. That's how come I'd never heard about him before." Sam and Lucille are glued to my every word. "His name is Stanley. And now he's back in Decatur because he's on this unbelievably dangerous mission."

"What kind of a mission?" Sam asks eagerly.

"Hold on, guys!" Lucille points to her watch. "It's almost eight. We've got to get back to Sam's before your parents show up, Charlie. Let's go."

Lucille, Sam, and I start running as fast as we can to the Endervelts' house. All I can think about is how brave my cousin was when he talked to me about leaving home. "My parents begged me to stay," he explained after I followed him into the thicket of trees just off the road. "But I knew it was for the best. And in the end they agreed with me: a creature should live with others of its kind."

"Sure thing," I agreed. I didn't want to tell Stanley that, except for Craig Dieterly and Amy Armstrong and a few other assorted creeps, I felt perfectly content living among humans. I didn't want him having second thoughts or anything. And he seemed to be so happy living in his creature-filled world. It actually did seem pretty cool.

"It's so great living under the lake," he said. "I have millions of friends who look just like me. And we go on all these amazing adventures in these hidden underwater prehistoric caverns together."

I can't even imagine how it must feel not to be the only green scaly giant around. Not that I would ever want to leave my two-legged family and friends. But still . . . it does make you wonder.

"Come on," Sam complains, shaking me out of my reverie. "I took the pledge and I want to know everything." He slows down to catch his breath. Lucille gives him a gentle nudge and he picks up the pace. "What's the creature's mission?" he pants.

"Here's the deal," I begin. "Stanley has been sent here to save his people from extinction from a deadly virus. The antidote is hidden somewhere in Decatur. He must find it and return home, or else . . ."

"Or else what, Charlie?" Lucille asks.

"All the mutant dinosaurs under Crater Lake will die a terrible death."

"That would be awful!" Sam says. We turn the corner at Maple and Euclid. We're almost at his house.

"It sure would," I answer. "And here's why it's *so* unbelievably important to keep his visit a secret." I lower my voice. "Stanley told me Aunt Harriet doesn't want anybody to know about it, but she has a really weak heart. And if she ever found out that he was up here, and what he was doing? She would probably have an attack or something."

"Wow," Lucille says, clearly impressed. "He must really trust you, Charlie."

"I'm one of his kind, guys. He knows he can count on me. He says that's why he sought me out: he knew I would never let him down."

"This is so exciting I can hardly stand it!" Lucille shrieks. "It makes *Forbidden Planet* look like *Sesame Street*."

"This is our best friend's relative we're dealing with here, Lucille," Sam explains. "It's not a movie or a TV show. We have a life-or-death situation on our hands. Get a grip."

"You're right," Lucille says softly. "I'm awfully sorry."

"Where is Stanley now, Charlie?" Sam asks.

"He's off looking for the antidote. He wouldn't tell me where. He can't tell anybody. I promised to bring him breakfast first thing in the morning, before school. And he promised he wouldn't go around stealing food anymore. And getting me into trouble."

We turn onto the Endervelts' block.

"Uh-oh, look who's here." Sam points to my mom's beat-up red pickup truck. It sits smack in the middle of Sam's driveway.

We are so busted it isn't even funny.

My mom storms out of Sam's house, followed by Sam's two unhappy-looking parents. "Let's go, Charles." Mom must be really mad. She never calls me Charles.

She yanks down the tailgate in the back of the truck

and I crawl in. "I've been scared to death. Where on earth have you been, Charlie?"

"I can explain," I begin.

"I certainly hope so," my mom says through clenched teeth. She hops into the front seat next to my dad. My father just sits there staring silently out the window. My parents don't say another word to me until we're home.

One we're settled in the kitchen, my mom really lays into me. "First of all, we know you weren't working on your English project because we called Mrs. Adams."

I sit at the kitchen table, staring at the floor, while my mom stands at the counter, making her famous high-fiber blueberry muffins. My dad stands next to her, helping stir the batter and looking really serious. "She says you handed in your project days ago."

"What? You talked to Mrs. Adams?" I practically shriek. "That is so embarrassing. Nobody's parents *ever* call their teachers."

"I'm really sorry, honey, but when I got to Sam's, you weren't there. Mrs. Endervelt said you told her you were at Lucille's house working on your English project. So I immediately called Naomi Strang, and when she told me you were at *Sam's* house working on your English project, we didn't know *what* to do." Mom pours the batter into a greased muffin tin.

My mom and Lucille's mom talk to each other ten zillion times a day. If a fly buzzes in Naomi Strang's kitchen, my mom hears about it two nanoseconds later.

"I don't understand what's going on, honey. We're worried about you. Is there something you want to tell us?" Mom asks, sticking the muffins into the oven. "Whatever's on your mind, just *say* it."

"You will never be punished for telling us the truth," my dad says. "I hope you know that, Charlie."

If only I could tell my parents. But I can't. The lives of thousands of creatures depend on it.

"I can't tell you," I finally say.

"Why?" My poor dad looks so confused.

"Because I made a promise that I wouldn't. I feel terrible, but you don't want me to go around breaking promises, do you guys?"

Mom thinks for a while before she answers. "I guess not. But we don't want you to go around keeping secrets from us, either."

"I don't know what else to do. It's nothing bad. I swear. I'll tell you when I can. You'll understand, I guarantee. Are you still mad at me?"

Mom shakes her head. "Your father and I aren't angry. Just disappointed."

Much later that night, after I've finished my homework and gone to bed, Dave finally tiptoes into our room. He was helping his favorite girlfriend, Janie, with her trig homework.

I'm still awake because I can't stop thinking about how cousin Stanley is on a death-defying mission to save the mutant dinosaurs of Crater Lake from extinction, and I can't even get it together to learn how to swim. "Hi, Dave," I say quietly. "I'm up."

"I noticed." My brother looks at me and scratches his head. "What's up?"

"I've got a lot on my mind."

He comes over and sits on the edge of my bed. "What is it, little bro?"

"I'm in trouble with Mom because I lied to her."

Dave reaches over and turns on my night light. "What did you lie about?"

"I told her I was going over to Sam's to study tonight. Only that's not what I was doing."

"What *were* you doing, Charlie?"

"Can't say."

"How come?"

"Promised I wouldn't."

"Who'd you promise?"

"Can't say."

I would love to tell Dave all about Stanley and his amazing quest, but my brother is the world's worst secret-keeper. He can't even keep what he's giving you for your birthday to himself. He doesn't mean to ruin surprises. It's just not in his nature to hide anything from anybody.

"I see your problem."

"I just feel so yucky when I lie, Dave. Especially to our parents."

"Lying is never a good thing, little bro. But I'm sure you had a perfectly good reason. And it's not like you were doing anything wild or crazy. . . . You weren't, right?"

"I don't do wild and crazy things, Dave. You know that. I'm just this incredibly boring mutant dinosaur who can't get anything right. I'm amphibious and I don't even know how to swim." I turn over on my side and stare glumly at the wall. "I'm such a loser."

"You keep telling yourself you're a loser, and pretty soon you'll convince yourself you really are one. And then you know what? You'll really *be* one, Charlie. And that would be a shame, you know?"

"Yeah. Right. Because I'm so terrific and amazing."

"No," Dave warns. "Because positive thoughts can build mountains and doubts can quickly tear them down."

Dave is always saying stuff like this to me. He says it's empowering. Basically it gives me a headache. He gets a lot of his material from *The Karate Kid*. He tried to make me watch it when I was nine. I fell asleep after the first three nanoseconds. It's his favorite movie. It's all about this kid who learns karate from a Zen master named Mr. Miyagi who goes around saying stuff like "Hope flies in on wings of despair" and "Inner peace will slay your outer dragon," and other expressions that I totally do not comprehend.

Dave hung the poster for the movie over his bed for inspiration. Sometimes he even talks to it before he goes to sleep. I myself prefer the original lobby card from George A. Romero's *Night of the Living Dead* starring Duane Jones and Judith O'Dea, which hangs over *my* bed. I never talk to it. I'm afraid it might say something back to me and I would jump out of my scaly green skin.

Dave reaches up and puts his arm around my slimy shoulders. "You're smart, you're funny, you're kind, you're unique. And I'm getting pretty tired of sitting around and listening to you telling yourself what you can't do. Start telling yourself what you *can* do for a change."

"Thanks for the advice, Dave. It's . . . uh . . . it's very helpful." I do not feel one iota better. But I can't tell Dave that, or he'll never stop talking. I yawn an enormous, fang-filled, seaweed-smelling yawn and stretch my stumpy arms.

"Great!" My brother reaches over and carefully pats the top of my cranial ridge. "'Night, little bro."

"'Night, Dave." He goes into the bathroom to wash up.

Balthazar pokes my stomach with his big brown nose and rolls over onto his back. I reach over and tickle his pale pink belly gently with my claws, and quicker than you can say "sometimes being twelve is like flying a single-engine airplane over the Rocky Mountains blindfolded without a parachute," I fall, exhausted, into a deep and troubled sleep.

Notes:

Order Junior Scientists' of America Detective Handbook

fire!

Take out trash tonight

Reminder:
DO NOT
EAT TRASH

Learn
how to
float

molten
lava

11
DON'T LOOK NOW

"SORRY I'M LATE, Doris. I can't get this darn collar to close." My dad races into the kitchen while Dave and I finish our egg-white omelets and gluten-free toast. Dad grabs his coffee cup and sticks out his neck, and my mom gets his shirt buttoned in about two nanoseconds. Dad sits down next to me and shoves a blueberry muffin into his mouth. Balthazar sits under the table eagerly licking up the crumbs at my dad's feet as they fall to the floor.

"Honey?" Mom clears her throat. Dad just sits there

chewing and sipping his coffee. "Wasn't there something you wanted to say, Fred?

Dad finally gets the hint, spits out a mouthful of coffee, and nearly chokes on his muffin. "I understand you're going through some difficulties, Charlie." He wipes his mouth with his napkin. "And, well, your mom and I . . . we were teenagers once ourselves, as hard as that may be for you to believe, and we know it can be quite a difficult and a challenging time. So . . ."

"Get to the point, Fred," Mom mutters under her breath. She hands Dave his lunch. He winks at me as he scoots out of the kitchen like a rat deserting a sinking ship. Great timing, Dave!

My dad swallows the rest of his muffin in one large gulp. "I want you to know your mother and I have given this a lot of thought, and after much discussion . . ."

"Your dad and I are going to be driving you to and from school for a while, honey," my mom finishes.

"It's not that we don't trust you, Charlie," my dad says. "It's just that—"

"We don't trust you, Charlie," my mom interrupts.

I slurp down my glass of OJ with my long pointy tongue and try not to panic. "I get where you're coming from." What am I going to do now? I have totally got to bring the poor creature his breakfast before I go to school because (A) I promised, and (B) if I don't, he'll just go out and steal more food, and I'll be in even more trouble.

"We called the Endervelts and the Strangs and said we'd be happy to drive Sam and Lucille, too. They'll be here any minute. Isn't that nice?" My mom pours my dad some more coffee.

"Yeah. Great." When everybody sees my parents driving me to school like I'm eight years old, I will never hear the end of it. I might as well just paint a sign on my back that says SHOOT ME NOW and get it over with.

The doorbell rings. My friends are here. "Let's go, sweetie!" My mom tosses her apron onto the counter. "Don't forget your backpack, Charlie!"

How could I forget it? I've got the creature's breakfast crammed into it: three jars of peanut butter, a loaf of bread, and all the canned tuna fish I could carry. It is so heavy I can barely hoist it onto my shoulder. I told Stanley I would meet him behind the rock outcropping at the corner of Cedar and Lonesome Lane on my way to school today. What do I do now?

My parents each hold one of my arms and escort me out to the driveway like a convicted felon.

"My mom says I can't go to the Junior Scientists of

America Jamboree in Wapakoneta, Ohio, next summer if I don't shape up," Lucille whispers as she helps me into the back of the truck.

"I'm under house arrest," I whisper back.

"Like we didn't notice," Sam says quietly as he climbs into the truck.

"Seat belts on, everybody!" my mom yells. We lurch noisily down the driveway and head for school. None of us wants anybody to see my parents driving us, so we scrunch way down and don't say a word the entire way.

When we get to school, we jump out of the truck and slink across the courtyard toward the front door, praying that none of the *nine trillion* Stevenson Middle School students pushing their way into the building will notice us. As if.

My mom shouts above the roar of the crowd: "Wait a minute, sweetie!"

It gets dead quiet as four hundred curious eyes turn to watch her get out of the truck and walk slowly up to me with outstretched arms.

My knobby knees grow weak at the horrifying possibility that my mother will kiss me good-bye in front of the entire Stevenson Middle School, grades five through eight. I can feel my score on the popularity chart plunging to record-breaking low levels with every step she takes until at last she stands before me. "You forgot something, honey." Everything turns into slow motion as she throws her arms around my massive neck and plants a big sloppy kiss on me. And then the entire middle school bursts into a round of spontaneous applause as she walks off, hops into the truck with my dad, and drives away like nothing happened.

As we enter the school lobby, Craig Dieterly and a bunch of Banditos and One-Upsters amble over to gloat.

"Cute, Swamp Thing, real cute!" My nemesis tries to tickle me under the chin, only fortunately he can't reach that high. "Does Mommy know her itty bitty baby monster is a thief and a liar?"

"Come on, Dieterly!" Lucille exclaims. "Charlie's innocent and you know it. There's no hard evidence."

"That's what *you* think, Strang." Craig Dieterly smiles malevolently. "There's been a new development in the case."

"You are in so much trouble it's crazy, Charlie Drinkwater." Rachel Klempner smiles gleefully. "It's so exciting I could burst. It's like I'm living inside of my own personal *CSI* episode and I am never ever going to change the channel as long as I live." She is practically salivating.

"What are you talking about?" I ask.

"They found a star witness," Craig Dieterly says. "You'll never guess who."

Sam, Lucille, and I exchange a worried glance.

"*My mother.* She saw you sneaking around Beautiful Bites yesterday afternoon carrying a carton of those pies right after the robbery. She was on her way to work at the hospital. She's a volunteer nurse on alternate Tuesdays. What do you have to say to that, Mr. McSlimy?"

Oh no! She must have spotted Stanley and thought it was me. I don't blame her. Even I can barely tell us apart.

Sam pulls himself up to his full four feet eleven and a half inches. "I say prove it, Dieterly."

"I say don't waste your breath, tubby." Amy Armstrong doesn't even bother to look up as she applies a perfect coat of smelly lacquer to her beautifully shaped nails. "Craig's mother is telling the truth. Last year Mrs. Dieterly received a letter of commendation from the American Medical Association. And they don't send letters of commendation to liars. So there." Amy Armstrong tosses her head and I am practically blinded by the sunlight reflecting off her golden curls. Then she laughs her adorable laugh and for one brief moment I almost forget how insincere she actually is.

"I didn't do it," I say. "I was home watching TV at the time of the break-in. I have witnesses." I point to Lucille and Sam.

"Your two loser friends would say anything to get you out of trouble and you know it, Mouse Breath."

Craig Dieterly snorts. "They don't count."

"That's not very nice," I protest.

"We're interesting." Amy Armstrong blows on her nails. "We don't have to be nice."

"That's right," Norm Swerling chimes in. "And after Craig's mom talks to Principal Muchnick, they'll be dragging your tail off to juvenile detention so fast you won't know what hit you." He cracks his gum for dramatic emphasis. I'm not exactly sure what juvenile detention is, but it doesn't sound good.

"What's Muchnick got to do with this?" I ask.

"Haven't you heard?" Rachel Klempner says a little too eagerly. "Principal Muchnick wasn't happy with the police investigation, so he started his own inquiry into the matter."

I get a sinking feeling in the pit of my very ample stomach. Now that an actual credible witness thinks they have seen me committing the crime, how will I ever get anyone to believe I didn't do it?

Craig Dieterly pushes me against the wall and starts twisting my shirt collar. "I didn't do it . . . I swear . . ." I struggle to catch my breath. "This is all . . . a terrible . . . mistake."

I spot Mr. Arkady watching us from the far end of the lobby. Norm Swerling says Mr. Arkady keeps a special coffin in his office for occasional daytime use when the sun gets too bright. Norm Swerling will basically say anything about anybody as long as it isn't nice.

"Are you calling my mother a liar?" Craig Dieterly pushes his big stupid face right into mine. "You take that back right now, or else I'll—"

"Or else you'll vutt, Meester Dieterly?" Our science teacher glides on over and intervenes. And not a moment too soon.

"Oh, never mind." Craig Dieterly skulks away. As he passes he murmurs to me, "Teacher's pet."

"Mr. Drinkvater." Mr. Arkady stares into my eyes intensely. "Let's have a leetle chat, shall vee?" He beckons me to follow him with a long, crooked finger. "Come vitt me." He swoops gracefully up the stairs to his office. I follow him, trying not to trip over my flippers and my eight-foot tail.

Maroon velvet drapes cover the windows and block out every shred of daylight in Mr. Arkady's inner sanctum. Row after row of small dead rodents and snakes floating in formaldehyde-laden glass jars line the shelves.

Stuffed ravens stare peacefully down at us from their concrete perches. I settle into an enormous chair that looks like it's made out of old bat wings and rat tails. It reminds me of a Bela Lugosi movie I saw when I was seven called *Murders in the Rue Morgue*. I like this place. I feel at home here. Mr. Arkady studies me closely. "How are tinks goink, yunk lizard?"

"Well, I'm sort of in trouble, actually, as you probably know, sir." I twiddle my claws nervously. All I can think about is how hungry poor Stanley must be as he goes through town, frantically looking for the antidote to save our relatives from extinction, and wondering why I deserted him this morning.

Mr. Arkady nods. "I haff heard a few tinks alonk the grapevine."

"Principal Muchnick forced me to be on the swimming team and I can't swim. Plus I'm a suspect in a series of robberies."

"I haff been vatchink the case vitt great interest."

"I'm innocent, sir, I swear!"

"Uff course you are, Charlie," Mr. Arkady quickly replies. "Anyvunn vitt half a brain knows dat."

I tap my flipper on the rug. I stare absentmindedly

at a row of stuffed weasels. "Plus . . . there's this other thing."

"Vatt other tink?" Mr. Arkady sits up in his chair and cocks his head to one side.

"I can't tell you," I say softly. I am dying to tell Mr. Arkady all about Stanley. He could probably even help find the antidote. Only I can't. Two years ago I told Mr. Arkady that Craig Dieterly had put the thumbtacks under Doc Craverly's tire. I asked him not to tell, but Mr. Arkady told Principal Muchnick anyway. Craig Dieterly figured out that it was me who snitched and he glued the top of my desk shut. I couldn't open it for the rest of the week.

No matter how much I would like to trust him, I must never forget that Mr. Arkady is, after all, still an adult.

"Speak up, yunk lizard. I can't hear you."

"I said, *I can't tell you.*"

"Vie not?" Mr. Arkady asks. He raises a pencil-thin eyebrow and gazes at me with his dark, piercing eyes.

"It's a secret. I can't tell *anyone.*"

"Ahhh." Mr. Arkady pulls his cape up around his pale, thin neck. "A secret. How intriguing." He rests his black-velvet-slipper-covered feet on the edge of his desk. His eyes twinkle and a faint smile crosses his thin, purplish lips. "A vell-kept secret ees a tiny mystery just vaitink to be solved. And I luff mysteries. As a yunk student I studied the complete vurks of Sir Arthur Conan Doyle. You know who dat is?"

"Yes, sir. He wrote the Sherlock Holmes novels. He was a forensic genius. *The Valley of Fear* is one of my favorite books."

"He vuss vitout a doubt the greatest mystery writer of all time. Dat book is the reason I became interested in science!" Mr. Arkady beams at me. "I read it venn I vuss a small boy-chick in Transylvania." He folds his long bony fingers in his lap and listens in rapt attention. "Vutt can I do for you?"

With every passing second Stanley is getting hungrier and more desperate. I can contain myself no longer. "Can you write me a permission slip to leave school this morning, Mr. Arkady?"

"Vutt?" He is taken aback at the request. He scrunches up his bat-wing-like shoulders and looks like he might fly away at any moment.

"I know it's a lot to ask. And I wouldn't if it weren't

very, very important. It won't take long. I'll be back in an hour. I swear."

"You vant my permission to leave school, but you von't tell me vie?"

"Well, I have this friend, you see, and he's . . . um . . . he's having some difficulties," I say very quietly. "No big deal."

"It sounds like a beeg deal to me," Mr. Arkady says. "Vutt kind of difficulties?"

"I'd rather not say."

"Hmm." Mr. Arkady's eyes glaze over and he stares into space. "This is a highly unusual rekvest," Mr. Arkady points out. "Your vurld ees an intriguing place, indeed, Mr. Drinkvater." He strokes his pointy chin. "I am inclined to trust you. You haff been through much adversity. And it has made you the better for it. You are goot boy, Charlie. I vill grant your request."

I breathe a sigh of relief. "Thank you, sir."

Mr. Arkady reaches out and rests two emaciated fingers on my shoulder. "I do not know vutt you are hidink. But I do know this: een this life, sometimes you must guard a secret vitt all your might. And sometimes you must set eet free and expose eet to the light of day.

I know all too vell vutt a burden it is to keep a secret," he continues. "I, too, svore to keep a secret for a friend many years ago, and I regret it to this day. Effry night the secret eats avay at me like a small mouse in my belly who is munching on a piece uff its favorite cheese vitt its needle-like teeth. Dat is a popular Transylvanian expression, in case you didn't know. Better, I say Mr. Drinkvater, nut to hide the truth. Be honest about yourself. And your friend. And vutt you are doink. In the end it vill be better for all concerned. Beeleef me."

"What's *your* secret, Mr. Arkady?" I ask, wide-eyed.

"I cannot tell you mine. Any more than you can tell me yours." Mr. Arkady smiles patiently. "You and I are honorable peoples. Vee keep our vurd. Vee are unusual."

"Thanks, Mr. Arkady."

"You are velcome, yunk lizard. And eef you are ever een doubt about vutt to do, let your heart be your guide, Charlie, and you vill alvays do the right tink. Remember these vurds. They vill serve you vell."

"I will, sir. I promise." I will definitely try to remember his words, but since I can never exactly make out what my science teacher is saying, it's going to be difficult to commit his actual words to memory.

"Goot!" My teacher picks up his ancient fountain pen and signs my permission slip with a flourish. "Here." He hands it to me.

"Thanks, Mr. Arkady." I tuck the little piece of paper carefully into my pocket.

"Good luck, yunk lizard."

"Thank you, sir." I get up to leave.

"Oh, and one more thing, Charlie."

I turn back quickly. "Yes, sir?"

"If you'd ever like a leettle help vitt your swimmink, don't be afraid to ask me. I used to be quite the athlete venn I vuss yunker. Now, get goink before I change my mind!" He smiles mischievously. With Mr. Arkady you can't always tell if he really means what he's saying or if he's just pulling your leg. Or your haunch, in my case.

I grab my backpack, throw on my jacket, and race downstairs. Doc Craverly sits quietly at his desk by the front door, drumming his fingers on his knee, looking bored. When he's not busy being the school psychologist, he doubles as the front door monitor.

I hand him my permission slip. He takes out his reading glasses and peers down at it. He couldn't be any slower if he tried.

"How's swimming practice going?" Doc Craverly asks.

"Not that well, sir."

"Would you like to talk to me about it privately sometime?" he asks eagerly.

"Not really, sir."

"Are you sure? I could probably squeeze in an appointment for you to see me sometime between now and . . . uh . . . pretty much anytime. Don't be shy." Poor Doc Craverly hardly has any patients. No one in their right mind would ever voluntarily see him.

"That's very kind of you, sir, but my schedule is pretty full right now. What with the big swim meet on Friday and all. Do you think you could sign my permission slip now?"

Doc Craverly takes out his pen, scribbles on it in what look like Egyptian hieroglyphics, and hands it to me. "If you change your mind, I have a free hour—"

I am out the door before he can finish the sentence.

I race to the rocky outcropping at Cedar and Lonesome. By the time I get there my side aches, and my enormous tongue is as dry as sandpaper. "I'm back!" I say softly, not wanting to create unnecessary attention.

Stanley doesn't respond.

"Come and get it!" I call in a considerably louder voice. Still no answer.

I carefully make my way behind the rocks, avoiding large roots and bits of crumbling sidewalk. I expect to find him hiding back there, not wanting to show himself in the daylight. But he's nowhere to be seen.

I sniff the air in search of his familiar musky odor, but there's an empanada festival in town this afternoon in honor of Pancho Villa Day, and the pungent aroma of spicy pork and cheese masks all but the most penetrating of odors. I carefully place Stanley's breakfast on top of a particularly flat rock, hoping he'll find it before some hungry raccoon does. Then I hurry back to school, distraught.

Stanley put his trust in me. And I failed him.

12

TELL IT TO THE JUDGE

SAM, LUCILLE, AND I huddle together on the little bench near the edge of the Stevenson Middle School playing field while two hundred middle schoolers race around, pushing, shoving, throwing food, and acting like a bunch of uncivilized maniacs. In other words: it's your basic recess.

"You're going to get an ulcer if you go around all day worrying like this," Sam tells me. "It's not healthy."

"Sam's right," Lucille agrees. "Stanley seems like a pretty capable creature. I'm sure he's okay."

"*I'm* not." I get up and start pacing. "And if something has happened to him, I'll never forgive myself."

"He'll be fine. He was fine before you found him, remember?" Sam is doing his best to calm me down, but it's having the opposite effect.

"That's easy for you to say. Thousands of innocent creatures aren't depending on *you* to complete a perilous mission. And what if he's out stealing more food? I'll get blamed and condemned to be on the swimming team for the rest of my life. I can't take the pressure any longer. I'm just a kid."

"Welcome to middle school, pal," Sam says.

"And just when I thought things couldn't get any worse . . . they can!" I announce when I see Principal Muchnick and Doc Craverly heading right for us.

"Quick!" Sam whispers. "Look innocent!"

"I *am* innocent," I say. My two least favorite adults in the entire school approach our little band of outcasts.

"Anything you say can and will be used against you in a court of law." Principal Muchnick pauses dramatically. "Do you understand, Mr. Drinkwater?" Doc Craverly stands beside him, sighing and wringing his hands.

"Yes, Principal Muchnick," I reply.

"Good." Principal Muchnick regards me thoughtfully and then suddenly turns on Doc Craverly. "Where's your notepad, man? I'm taking a deposition. Shape up. What are you planning to write on, the back of your hand?"

Doc Craverly reaches into his coat pocket and digs deeply into it. At last he pulls out a small, dog-eared notepad and pencil.

"Listen up, Drinkwater. Do you swear to tell the truth, the whole truth, and nothing but the truth, so help you God?"

"I do." As I speak several Banditos and One-Upsters come over to see what's up.

"Where were you on the afternoon of November eleventh between the hours of four thirty and five fifteen? Think hard. Your exact whereabouts, Drinkwater."

"Can you speak a little slower please, Willard?" Doc Craverly whispers urgently. "I'm having trouble keeping up with the pace of the interrogation." He massages his right hand with his left. "Plus, I'm developing a painful cramp in my writing finger."

"Tough it up, Craverly," Principal Muchnick barks.

"What do you think this is, SUMMER CAMP???" He walks up to me until we are practically nose to snout. "Your whereabouts at the time of the crime, Drinkwater. Answer, please."

"He was watching *Invasion of the Body Snatchers* with us," Sam says.

"That's right," Lucille adds. "He wouldn't have had time to commit the crime."

Mr. Muchnick points his finger at me. "Are you trying to tell me that you did not steal three cases of freshly baked sugar-free cherry pies and a box of low-fat soy cheese croissants from Mr. Hollabird's establishment?"

I nod my head emphatically.

"Why would Charlie rob a person who was considering carrying a line of his mom's baked goods?" Lucille asks. "It doesn't make any sense."

Craig Dieterly steps forward. "Don't listen to Lucille, Principal Muchnick. She'll say anything to protect her friend. My mother is the only believable eyewitness in the entire case. You had her in your office for half an hour. She positively identified Charlie. Don't you think it would be a good idea to at least punish him?"

"Slow down, everybody!" Doc Craverly cries. "I

can't keep up with you. I've broken the tip of my pencil. I'm losing critical information here."

"I DON'T GIVE A FLYING FLOUNDER!" Principal Muchnick tosses the poor psychologist a new pencil.

"I'm afraid Charlie is going to go on robbing the town blind unless you do something to stop him, Principal Muchnick." Craig Dieterly is red in the face. "I'm really worried!"

The only thing Craig Dieterly is really worried about is that he won't make my life miserable enough. And there isn't much chance of that.

All eyes turn to Principal Muchnick. His greasy black hair falls in messy strands onto his forehead. Even his usually meticulous three-piece pin-striped suit is starting to show signs of wear and tear. His collar droops unevenly around his neck, and a dark sweat stain is forming on his jacket under each of his armpits.

Principal Muchnick wipes his brow with a crumpled handkerchief from his vest pocket and studies me intently. "Every great leader occasionally reaches a point in a critical situation where he or she becomes overwhelmed from too much information and too many opinions. It's part of the job. In the end all that you can do is wait for the dust to settle and rely on your instincts. And your nose for justice."

Doc Craverly smiles at Principal Muchnick and eagerly nods his approval.

"What are you nodding about, Craverly?" Principal Muchnick barks. "You look ridiculous. Stop it immediately."

Doc Craverly stares at his feet sheepishly.

Principal Muchnick continues. "I have reached such a point. And it is not a happy place." He shakes his head. Little beads of grease mixed with sweat fall onto the ground around him.

Norm Swerling raises his hand. Principal Muchnick nods. "For the record, Drinkwater isn't trustworthy. He cheats in swimming practice."

"Norm's right," Dirk Schlissel agrees. "My brother and I watched him with our own four eyes the other day. He pretended to be swimming, but he was *walking*. We hate to say it, Principal Muchnick, but we don't really think Charlie Drinkwater's all that honest."

I can stay silent no longer. "That's not true, Principal Muchnick! I strenuously object to these unfounded allegations of malfeasance."

"Could you make Drinkwater speak in English,

Principal Muchnick?" Dack Schlissel asks. "We can't understand a word he's saying."

It is very painful to hear myself talked about like this because (A) I am so trustworthy it isn't funny. Look at how far I'm going just to keep Stanley's secret! And (B) I only walked in the pool the other day because I was afraid I would drown if I swam. That's not being dishonest. That's just being careful.

"They're just jealous of Charlie!" Lucille exclaims. "Don't listen, Principal Muchnick. They'd do anything to get him in trouble."

"Like we could ever be jealous of Charlie Drinkwater," Larry Wykoff says smugly. "That's like being jealous of wallpaper. Forget it. Not happening." Rachel Klempner looks adoringly up at her own personal king of comedy.

"There's more to life than just getting good grades and doing well on standardized testing," Norm Swerling says. "Like having good morals, for example."

Norm Swerling wouldn't know a good moral if it walked up to him and bit him on the nose. Boy, would I like to tell that stupid Bandito what I really think. And that is exactly what I'd do if I weren't so afraid to do it.

Fear number twelve thousand and one: standing up for myself.

"Bigot!" Sam yells at the top of his lungs. "You people don't like lizards and amphibians and you never did. Admit it!"

"Thief!" Alice Pincus hollers, pointing a tiny finger at me.

"Quiet!" Principal Muchnick's piercing voice cuts through the noise like shattering glass. "I can't hear myself think!" He looks up and speaks slowly and calmly. "Something fishy is going on here. This much I know: somebody isn't telling the truth and I'm inclined to think it's you, Mr. Drinkwater. While I find Sam and Lucille's testimony compelling, as your best friends they are not entirely impartial, and could have sufficient reason to lie on your behalf."

Craig Dieterly raises his fist and churns the air triumphantly.

"On the other hand, Mr. Dieterly," the principal goes on, "though your mother is known to be a scrupulously honest woman and is undoubtedly telling what she believes to be the truth, eyewitnesses do make mistakes. Your mother is extremely nearsighted, is she not?"

"Well . . . yes," Craig Dietelry reluctantly admits. "But I don't understand what that has to with anything, Principal Muchnick."

"Does she or does she not frequently misplace her eyeglasses, Mr. Dieterly?"

"Um . . . well . . ." Craig Dieterly hesitates. "I wouldn't say *frequently*."

"What *would* you say, Mr. Dieterly?" Doc Craverly utters harshly.

"Back off, man," Principal Muchnick orders. "You're intimidating the witness."

"I'd say it was more like . . . um . . . occasionally." A bead of sweat runs down Craig Dieterly's monkeylike forehead.

"And was she or was she not wearing them on the day of the robbery?" Principal Muchnick asks.

"She was not," Craig Dieterly quietly admits. A murmur arises from the crowd.

"The testimony of the defendant's best friends on the one hand," Principal Muchnick begins, "and a seeing-impaired eyewitness, who just happens to be the plaintiff, on the other. All of which leaves me rather perplexed at the moment." He loosens his collar. "But as my uncle Eddie Muchnick, the ex–chief of police of our great city, once said, 'A crime is nothing more than an elaborate jigsaw puzzle whose interlocking pieces are spread before you in a random fashion on a large table. One has only to arrange them in the proper order to see the whole picture.' Have no fear. I will assemble the pesky pieces of this puzzle before the week is out. I *always* get my man."

Principal Muchnick stamps his foot in the grass with such force his shoe gets stuck in the dirt and Doc Craverly has to get down on his hands and knees to help him pull it out.

I can feel the noose tightening. It is only a matter of time before Principal Muchnick apprehends the *real* criminal. If Stanley doesn't accomplish his mission soon, I may have to confess to the crime myself and face the consequences in order to buy my brave cousin a little more time.

13
MISSING IN ACTION

AS SOON AS the end-of-the-day bell rings, I race downstairs to see if Stanley is anywhere in the vicinity. I'm hoping he picked up my scent and followed it to school. I check out the tangle of bushes next to the science lab and look carefully behind all the Dumpsters near the cafeteria. I sniff the air in every direction. But Stanley is nowhere to be smelled. I'll have to go looking for him when my parents aren't around. Only my mom won't let me out of her sight for a second. This is going to be difficult.

I'd better come up with a plan, and fast. But for now, I go join my friends on the front steps.

"Any sign of your cousin?" Lucille asks as soon as she sees me.

"Not a trace." I sigh. "I sure hope he's okay."

"Want me and Sam to go look for him after your mom drops us off? We could try to attract him with my tuna fish sandwich. I saved it from lunch."

"That's very kind of you to offer, Lucille," I answer. "But Stanley won't come out if there are humans around."

"How come?" Lucille asks.

"Because he's afraid we might tell Aunt Harriet he's here and she could drop dead of a heart attack, remember?" Sam has a great memory for details.

"Yeah, but we took the Mainframe pledge," Lucille replies. "We would never tell anyone."

"But Stanley doesn't *know* that, Lucille. I'm the only one who can find him," I insist. "He trusts me. I'm one of his kind."

I hear my mom's old truck backfiring in the distance.

"What are you going to do?" Lucille asks.

"I don't know. Wait for everybody to go to sleep tonight and then go look for him, I guess," I reply.

"That's pretty adventurous of you, pal," Sam remarks.

"Don't remind me, Sam. I don't really have much of a choice. I'll bring him dinner and do everything I can to help him find the antidote. If he'll let me. If I can find him."

"That's a lot of ifs," Sam comments.

"Yeah," I say simply. "I know." I stare at the driveway and chew nervously on the tips of my claws until my mom's truck finally rattles and wheezes up to the front of the school. "Let's go, guys. The parent police are here."

Before you can say "getting picked up after school by your mother is the fastest way known to man to lower your score on the popularity chart," we have dropped off Sam and Lucille at their houses, and I have finished my homework, eaten dinner, and watched half of *Revenge of the Nerds*, one of my very favorite nonscary movies, on TV.

Now it's after ten and I lie motionless in my bed like a butterfly pinned to a sheet of foam core. I am waiting for everyone else in my family to fall asleep while the worries of the day swirl madly around in my head.

I wonder if I'll find Stanley in time to help him

locate the antidote, or if Principal Muchnick will find him first. I wonder if I will survive my next swimming practice, which is only eighteen hours and ten minutes away (but who's counting?). I wonder what new ways Craig Dieterly will find to torture me, and how rejected Amy Armstrong and her One-Upsters will make me feel tomorrow at school. "Fear of rejection." That's a big one in my book. It's right up there with "fear of stepping on a rusty nail and getting lockjaw." Don't laugh. It happens.

To make the time pass more quickly, I mentally list animals that seem basically harmless but could suddenly attack you when you least expect it. I am up to "overly aggressive pigeons" when Dave finally tiptoes into our room and gets into his pj's.

"Are you asleep, little bro?" He gets into bed and turns out the night light.

"Not exactly."

"Worried about swimming practice, huh?"

"Yes," I reply. *Among other things*, I add to myself.

"You'll do fine, little bro."

"Easy for you to say. You're the sports champion of the galaxy."

Dave laughs. "Remember, sport: 'When we push the

immovable object up the hill slowly, we encounter our true inner self quickly.'"

"That's a very thought-provoking...um...thought," I reply. "And I'm sure it will come in extremely handy one day. If I can ever figure out what it means. Can you give me a hint, Dave? Practice is tomorrow and I'd love a little nugget of wisdom to hold on to that might possibly prevent me from drowning. How about it? Earth to Dave . . . Earth to Dave . . . come in, Dave. . . ."

My brother doesn't reply. His steady breathing turns into loud rhythmic snoring. Balthazar curls up at the foot of my bed and rests his big, black, shaggy head on my flippers. Even Dave's tropical fish seem to be settling down for the night in their softly gurgling tank on his bookshelf.

I, on the other hand, am totally awake and ready to spring into action. I slip out of bed, careful not to wake up either my furry roommate or the other one, and quietly shuffle out of my room and into the hallway. I press my earflap up to my parents' door. I hear my dad's snoring and my mom's quiet, even breathing. The TV is off. The white noise machine is on. All systems go.

I make my way downstairs, careful not to make a sound. I even breathe quietly. Then I step on one of Balthazar's old squeak toys. Oh no.

I freeze for several heart-stopping moments until I am absolutely convinced no one has heard me. And then I move silently through the back hallway and into the kitchen. I feel like a cat burglar.

I stick some leftovers into a Tupperware container, grab a couple of paper napkins, and then, certain that no one is up and about, I open the back door. Suddenly the Tupperware slips out of my claws. I try to grab it, but it falls to the ground with a resounding clatter.

If my parents wake up and find me sneaking out of the house in the middle of night, they will ground me for the rest of my life. I should have left them a note. I could have said I got a cramp in my thigh and was going outside to walk it off.

I shouldn't be doing this. Good kids don't sneak out of the house at eleven o'clock on a school night.

No, I *should* be doing this. It's good to come to the aid of your fellow . . . um . . . creature in need.

Fear number twelve thousand and three: not doing the right thing.

I slowly back into the yard and look up at my parents' window, expecting to see their lights snap on at any second. But fortunately all remains dark on the second floor. At least for now.

Suddenly I catch a distinct whiff of mutant dinosaur. I wheel around to see Stanley leaning against the side of the garage, waiting for me. His scales sparkle in the glow of the faint yellow path lights that line the driveway. It is oddly reassuring to find myself in the presence of my own kind.

"Nice to see you, Charlie," Stanley whispers hoarsely, waving a claw at me. He doesn't seem mad at me for not getting him his food on time this morning. That's a relief.

"Nice to see you too, Stanley. How are you doing?" If you had ever told me I'd be making small talk with my mutant dinosaur cousin in my very own backyard at eleven o'clock at night, I would have said you were crazy.

"Tired. Very tired." He yawns a huge yawn, and looks like he might keel over any minute. "And extremely hungry."

"I'm so sorry. I couldn't shake my parents this morning. And then when I finally did, you weren't there, and I couldn't find you anywhere, and . . ."

Fear number twelve thousand and four: fear of being blamed.

"Relax. It's okay. I figured something came up. Don't look so worried, friend. I didn't steal any food. I made do with earthworms and wild berries. I didn't want you getting into any more trouble on my account."

"Thanks." There is a real bond forming between us. I can feel it as clearly as I feel the fog rolling in and blanketing the yard and the street behind it. "Here." I hand him the Tupperware container. "It's leftovers. I hope you like Chinese food."

He nods eagerly and dumps the entire contents into his gaping jaws. His meal slithers down his throat in one enormous gulp. Some stray bits of moo goo gai pan ooze out from between his fangs. His long, pointy tongue whips around like an eggbeater, slurping it all up. "I forgot what a good cook your mom is."

"Where have you been today, Stanley? I was worried."

"I'm really not supposed to talk about it. I'm lucky to be alive." He sighs. "You wouldn't believe what I've been through. But it looks like the mission is going to be a success."

"That's great!" I hand him a napkin. He wipes the grease from his snout.

"Thanks."

"How'd you find my house ?" I ask.

"I used to come here all the time. I babysat for you when you were two. I'm your cousin, remember?" Stanley seems to have perked up considerably since finishing the leftovers. He burps loudly and turns to leave.

"Where are you going?"

"I'm taking you to Crater Lake for your swimming lesson like I said I would. What do you say?"

I stand there, flippers firmly glued to the ground, terrified at the prospect.

"What's the matter?" he asks.

"I didn't . . . um . . . realize you were going to . . . actually . . . you know . . ."

"Follow through?"

I nod.

"I generally do what I say I'm going to do, Charlie. It's an old habit of mine."

"Yeah . . . but . . . but don't you have more important

things to do? Like saving the lives of thousands of infected creatures?"

"Not right now. I'm in pretty much of a holding pattern for the next few hours. What do you say, Charlie? Feel like conquering some of your swimming demons?"

Why can't I be more like Stanley? He was in life-threatening danger today, and he's not even thinking about it. Stanley's not afraid of anything. I bet he *loves* tapioca pudding. He probably sprinkles palmetto bugs on top.

But I'm afraid of everything. I have been ever since I can remember. I'm afraid a polar bear will escape from the zoo and eat me. (It happens. Polar bears are ingenious.) I'm afraid of being alone in my room at night. I'm afraid of loud noises. I'm afraid of Craig Dieterly. I'm afraid people will laugh at me. I'm afraid people *won't* laugh at me.

Maybe it's time to stop being so afraid.

"Sure. Let's go."

I look around to see who said that. It was me.

14

SPLISH-SPLASH

STANLEY AND I stay off the sidewalk and hide behind the trees by the side of the road as we make our way to Crater Lake. Stanley doesn't want to be seen any more than I do. We take the shortcut through the ravine. Nobody ever goes there.

"What's it like under Crater Lake?" I ask.

"It's not all that different from Decatur, actually," Stanley answers. "Only everybody looks like us, of course. And there aren't any sidewalks."

"Do we have a lot of relatives down there?"

"Oh yeah. You can hardly swim down the street without bumping into one of us. Nana Wallabird had ten brothers and sisters, and they all had kids. And their kids had kids. Nearly fifty of them showed up at my last birthday party."

"Sounds nice." I really love my Decatur family. And a creature couldn't ask for better friends than Sam and Lucille. But I can't even imagine what it must feel like to look like everybody else. And not get stared at all the time. And wear regular clothes that your mom doesn't have to make you.

We walk until my neck aches and my flippers are sore. Finally we reach the outskirts of Decatur. And still we keep walking. There are no streetlights out here. Not many houses, either. Instead row after and row of towering pine trees, and pin oaks as far as the eye can see. The sidewalk has turned into a small, winding dirt path. Luckily there's a crescent moon peeking through the clouds, so it's not hard to find our way. I sense the dampness in the air. We must be getting close.

"Look." Stanley points. "There it is!"

Crater Lake looms in the distance. The engraved copper plaque on the bank explains: "Crater Lake was formed over sixty million years ago, during the Cretaceous period, when a meteor landed and wiped out most of the living things on earth."

Most people's ancestors came to America from places like Europe. Or Asia. Or Africa. Mine came from the bottom of Crater Lake.

Once when I was ten my dad took me and my brother boating here and we saw a rare blue heron taking off from its nest near the shoreline. Dave and I got so excited we stood up and tipped over the canoe and my dad had to rescue me. By the time he dragged me to shore, I had swallowed so much water he had to perform artificial respiration on me. I was fine afterward. But I never forgot what it felt like. And I never went anywhere near Crater Lake again.

Until tonight.

"What are you thinking about, Charlie?" Stanley asks.

"Drowning . . . and carnivorous insects . . . and poisonous fish . . . and having the vital fluids sucked out of my body by dozens of bloodthirsty vampire leeches. You know . . . the usual stuff."

"I'm sorry I asked." Then Stanley makes a mad dash for the water. "Lake, here I come!"

When he gets to the shoreline, he dives right in and disappears under the surface for what seems like an eternity. I run breathlessly to the edge and peer out into the inky black deep, looking for him. Suddenly he catapults into the cold night air. His enormous scaly body hangs above the surface of the lake, shimmering in the moonlight for one magical instant, then plunges back down, disappearing again into the inky black water

I hover nervously by the shore and wait for Stanley to resurface. His scaly green head pops up about twenty yards away from me. He waves cheerfully and heads back

to me. When it gets too shallow to swim, he stands up and walks on over. "Ready for your first lesson, Charlie?"

No, if you really want to know the truth. But I can't disappoint Stanley. He seems so excited. And I really do trust him. Plus, I've already come this far. I step out of my pj's and carefully wade out to join him until the water is lapping at my knees. Stanley reaches for me. I grab on to him for dear life.

"Easy, Charlie, you're cutting off the circulation in my right claw." I hold on a little less tightly, still afraid to let go altogether. "Don't worry," my cousin tells me gently. "I'm practically a professional. I've taught so many creatures how to swim by now it isn't funny. Ouch! Can you be a little more careful with your claw there?"

"Sorry." I loosen my grip some more. "What do we do now?"

"We go deeper," my cousin says simply.

I stare out at the vast expense of murky water ahead and wish I'd never even heard of Stanley O'Connor.

"How am I going to teach you how to swim if you won't get in the water, Charlie? Just a little farther. Come on. It won't kill you."

"That's what *you* think." I hold my breath and take a few tentative steps into the lake. The water feels so . . .

wet. The sand squishes under my flippers and sticks to the spaces between my webbed toes.

I hold on to Stanley's claw and we continue walking until the water is up to my neck. I experience a desperate urge to flee. Which I would happily do at this exact moment, only I don't want to act like a whiny baby in front of my ultrabrave cousin, so instead I keep walking until I am standing on the very tips of my flippers and struggling to keep my head above the water. That's when I begin to hyperventilate. "Great swimming lesson, Stanley. Thanks so much. This is where I get off."

"Are you kidding? We're just getting started. You can't quit now, Charlie. You're doing great."

I am getting extremely dizzy from the accumulation of CO_2 in my bloodstream.

"It's too deep. I can't stand. I'm not happy. I want to go home." I feel the way I felt when my brother tried to teach me how to ride my two-wheeler. Only falling off a bike and scraping my knee on the pavement was nowhere near as terrifying as the prospect of sudden death by drowning.

"The water isn't your enemy, Charlie. It's your friend."

"Try telling that to the water." I turn around and

start racing back to shore on the tips of my flippers like a giant, crazed, green ballet dancer.

"Okay. If that's what you want, we'll leave now. I just sort of thought you might enjoy learning how to swim. That's all." He looks so disappointed.

Against my better judgment and a thousand warning signs blinking in my head that say, DANGER AHEAD TURN BACK NOW SAVE YOURSELF WHILE YOU CAN, I walk slowly back to my cousin and take hold of his claw again. "Can we get this over with quickly? I don't know how much more of this swimming business I can handle."

"Hold on to me with both claws, close your eyes, and relax," Stanley announces. At this point I don't have sufficient energy left to protest, so I let my cousin walk me farther out into the water while I concentrate on staying alive. "Turn over, Charlie." I wriggle onto my back. "Good work, cuz."

What choice do I have? With floating you're either above the water and doing fine, or you're sinking and you're not. There isn't a lot of in between.

"Remember to breathe slowly and evenly," Stanley says. "In . . . out . . . in . . . out." The lack of oxygen, the gentle rippling effect of the water as it rushes past my

scaly body, and Stanley's soothing voice have a decid-
edly calming effect on me. I float gracefully along the
surface, bobbing gently up and down like an enormous
scaly green cork.

"In . . . out . . . in . . . out . . ." Stanley continues.

"Can we go home now?"

"I hate to burst your bubble, cuz," Stanley says
proudly, "but you're on your own, and you're doing just
fine."

What's he talking about? I turn my pointy head
around and notice that my cousin has let go of my claws
entirely. That's funny. No one is holding me up, and
nothing bad seems to be happening.

For one brief moment, I consider the amazing possibility that I may actually have just learned how to
swim . . . and then I look down into the water and it
dawns on me that this is the deepest lake in all of southern Illinois. And that if I were to somehow forget what
I was doing, I could actually drown. Alarm bells go off
deep in the recesses of my brain. Every muscle in my
body tenses up.

I tell myself to relax, but it's way too late for anything as sensible as that. I open my enormous jaws to

tell Stanley to please hold me up, I am having difficulty staying afloat, but a piercing scream emerges instead. I splutter. I flail. I gasp. I take in water and start to choke.

Stanley tries to hold on to me, but I am thrashing around so violently he cannot possibly get a good grip. I promptly begin sinking like a stone.

Down and down, faster and faster I go, like Alice in Wonderland tumbling helplessly down the rabbit hole. I am weak from holding my breath. And numb with fear.

I always thought my entire life would flash before my eyes before I died. But as I hurtle downward through the icy water, I see exactly one thing: Craig Dieterly. His stupid fat face and giant horse teeth loom in front of me, larger than life. He is laughing so hard he can barely catch his breath. He gasps for air. Coughing and spluttering.

I realize the sound I hear is me desperately trying to breathe.

I am growing weaker by the second. I feel the life draining out of my body. With every last fiber of my exhausted being I struggle to remain conscious. I can't hold on much longer.

My lungs are about to burst when Stanley finally gets hold of me. In my desperation, I strike at him with my claws and powerful legs and try to escape. But he won't give up. He just holds on tighter and wrestles me back to the surface.

We break through the surface and the cold night air hits me in the face, shocking me back into consciousness. Stanley drags my limp body out of the water and back onto shore. He turns me onto my stomach and pushes on my back with all his might, and water comes pouring out of my lungs like a fountain. He keeps pushing until there isn't any more, and I sprawl on the ground, waiting for my strength to return.

At last I open my eyes and look around, dazed. "Are you okay?" Stanley asks. I open my jaws to speak, but nothing comes out. "Talk to me, Charlie."

"I . . . don't . . . know." I attempt to stand, but my legs give way. I collapse to the ground in a heap.

Stanley grasps my spindly arms. "One, two, three, go!" he grunts, and together we struggle until at last I am standing upright. "I'm sorry, Charlie." Stanley says quietly. "I'm so sorry."

"It wasn't your fault. I can't swim and I never will."

I slip back into my pj's and we start the long trek back. Stanley doesn't let go of my arm until we reach the corner of Lonesome Lane and Cedar Street.

"Think you can make it the rest of the way on your own?" he asks.

"I'll be fine," I answer. "What about you, Stanley?"

"Don't worry about me. I can take care of myself."

"I'll leave your breakfast on the tree stump behind the garage in the morning. And your dinner tomorrow night, too. I won't forget, Stanley. I promise."

"I know." My cousin turns and disappears into the fog, a brave lonely figure in the dark.

My legs won't stop shaking. Every muscle in my body aches. In less time than it takes to say "I am never going into the water again as long as I live," I am tiptoe-ing into my bedroom, slipping into my warm cozy bed, and dreading the swimming practice that awaits me in only fifteen short hours.

Notes:

H^1

Mjölnir

Learn the
periodic table
for extra credit
science report

Zn^{30}

Ca^{20}

Check out
meteor shower

Buy fake
rubber dog poo
to drive my
parents crazy!

Learn how to
Swim or ELSE!!

15

WATER, WATER, EVERYWHERE

EVER HEAR OF "Drinkwater's theory of relativity"? I didn't think so. It's sort of like Einstein's theory of relativity. Only not as well-known. I came up with it last year while waiting in Nurse Nancy's office for my tetanus booster, and I only told two other people in the entire solar system. Right. Sam and Lucille. Here's how it goes:

Time expands in proportion to how much you are looking forward to something. It contracts in proportion to how much you are dreading it.

Here's how it works. Pick a time period. Any time period. Like today, for example. The actual time that elapsed between the beginning of my first-period science class and the beginning of my horrible, terrible, stupid, terrifying, end-of-day swimming practice, as measured by the clock in the cafeteria, was exactly six and a half hours.

The relative time? Less than five minutes. I might as well have been hurtling through space in Han Solo's spaceship at a velocity surpassing the speed of light; that's how fast it went.

And now the hour of doom is upon me. I trudge dejectedly down the stairs like I am on my way to my own funeral. Which, come to think of it, I sort of am. Because when I refuse to go into the water today, Coach Grubman is going to kill me. And if *he* doesn't, Principal Muchnick will.

"You are valkink very slowly, Mr. Drinkvater," Mr. Arkady observes when he spots me.

"I'm on my way to swimming practice, Mr. Arkady."

"Let me congratulate you," he says. "You are doink a magnificent job of not gettink there."

"Thanks."

"I vuss hopink you verr becomink more accustomed to the water, Mr. Drinkvater." He strokes his long, pointy chin with his bony hand.

"No such luck, I'm afraid," I reply, thinking about last night with a shudder.

"You vill. Don't worry. You'll see." Mr. Arkady looks at me sympathetically. "On a scale of one to ten, how hard vuss it for you to ace your science midterm the udder day?"

"One, I guess," I reply. "I do well on tests."

"Why is that?" Mr. Arkady asks.

"I never really thought about it. It just comes naturally, I guess."

"And so vill svimmink, yunk lizard. Venn you let it."

"What do you mean, sir?" I glance at the clock on the wall. The end-of-day bell is going to ring any second. Practice is about to start. I twiddle my claws and shift about anxiously on my very large flippers.

"You come from a lonk line of vater-lovink creatures. You do nut haff to learn to *svim*. You haff to learn nut to *stop* yourself from svimmink. Eet ees een your DNA."

I think Mr. Arkady just gave me some really good

advice about swimming. Only I could barely understand a word he said. But before I have a chance to ask him to repeat himself, the bell rings.

I race into the hallway and tear down the back stairs to the locker room. I've got to get to practice early so Craig Dieterly and his Bandito friends won't be there to make fun of me when I change into my bathing suit. I dash down the basement corridor and into the boys' locker room. Great! Nobody's here yet. I rip off my clothes, shove them into an open locker, and throw on my bathing suit before anyone arrives.

I walk slowly out of the locker room and stare at the Olympic-sized pool that lies before me. The combined odor of chlorine and mildewed towels hits me in the snout like a cement pillow. "Never going in. Never going in. Never going in." Let them yell at me. Let Coach Grubman wheedle and threaten and complain. How much more can my teammates hate me than they already do? I am *never going in*.

Speaking of my teammates: where is everybody? It's much too quiet in here. I don't hear any shoving and pushing. Craig Dieterly's obnoxious laughter doesn't echo through the tiled cavernous space like a delirious hyena. No one's even making farting sounds with his cupped hand and his underarm. It's unnerving.

Suddenly wet feet slap against the tiled floor. I quickly turn to see every one of the fifteen Sardines lined up behind me in a solid phalanx. No one says a thing. They just lock arms and walk slowly, inexorably toward me, like those terrifying townspeople who have had their brains scooped out in *Invasion of the Body Snatchers*.

What do they think they're going to do, push me in? I'll yell for Coach Grubman and he'll come to my rescue. Coach might not like me all that much, but he can't exactly afford to have a student drown during swimming practice, either. Which is when I start to feel relieved. Which is when it dawns on me that Coach Grubman is nowhere to be seen.

I know this because when I holler "COACH!!!!!" at the top of my mighty lungs, not one single person comes running out of the locker room to stop them.

"Save your breath, Swamp Thing." Craig Dieterly doesn't even bother to raise his voice. "It's just you and us," he says, gesturing to the other Banditos, who continue their steady march toward me. "Coach Grubman isn't here to save you this time."

"Yes, he is," I insist feebly. "He's about to open the door any second. Oh wow. Listen to that." I cock my pointy head to one side. "Here he comes now. I can hear him with my superpowerful creature hearing."

"No, you can't," Norm Swerling murmurs.

"Oh yeah? How do *you* know?" I try to sound tough and brave. But all I really sound is scared and little. Which, considering I am eight and a half feet tall and weigh over seven hundred and fifty pounds, is something of an accomplishment.

"Because Coach Grubman put a note into our cubbies saying he'd be fifteen minutes late for practice today, only somehow you never got yours," Dirk or Dack Schlissel says smugly.

Craig Dieterly smiles cheerfully. "Say, what's this I see in my bathing suit?" Dieterly pulls out a wadded-up, soggy piece of paper and unfolds it. "It's got your name on it, Minnow Mouth." He holds it up and waves it at me. "What do you know? It's a note from Coach Grubman." I don't even bother to look. "Hey, Drinkwater, are you ready for a nice refreshing dunk? Heads up, fellow Sardines. On the count of three we play 'push the creature into the pool.' Ready, everyone? On your mark . . . get set . . ."

"Please don't. I'm begging you. I can't swim."

"What did you say?" Craig Dieterly cups his ear. "I can't hear you," he taunts.

"He said he can't swim," Larry Wykoff whispers urgently. "I don't know if this is such a good idea, guys. It could be really dangerous."

"I'm going to pretend I didn't hear you, Wykoff." Craig Dieterly glares viciously at him. "Everybody, man your battle stations and . . . *go!!!*"

My teammates gather around and start pushing me toward the dreaded pool. I push back as hard as I can, but my flippers slip and slide on the tiled floor, and within seconds I crash into the deep end.

The team cheers wildly as my head sinks beneath the water. I reach blindly for the edge of the pool, coughing and spluttering, until I get a firm grip with one of my claws.

I take a deep, satisfying gulp of air. And then another one. But Craig Dieterly and the Schlissel twins try to pry my claws loose. I am about to slip back into the water when Coach Grubman races into the room shouting, "What's going on here?"

"If you tell on us you're done for, so don't even think about it," Craig Dieterly whispers furiously into my earflap.

Coach Grubman's rubber band is spinning around his hands so fast you can barely see it. "It's unsafe to go into the water without an adult present. You should know better. I'm surprised at you, Drinkwater," he barks. "Do you hear me?"

"But Coach . . . you don't understand . . . I didn't do anything. I was just . . ."

"I don't want to hear another word."

"We told him not to go in, but he wouldn't listen to us, Coach," Craig Dieterly lies.

"*Enough!!!*" Coach grabs my shoulders and helps drag my enormous bulk from the pool. "You will remain silent and stay out of trouble for the rest of practice. Do I make myself perfectly clear?"

"Absolutely, sir." So I lie by the side of the water and watch as Coach blows three ear-splitting blasts into his whistle. Evidently this is some kind of secret code for people who understand whistle-blowing because everybody springs into action and runs around choosing teams.

Within nanoseconds, four groups of Sardines are eagerly lined up along the deep end of the pool while I watch, numbly, from the tiled floor. Swimmer after swimmer completes his qualifying rounds for tomorrow's big meet against the Carbondale Catfish.

Finally Coach Grubman blows another couple of blasts on his whistle. It must be the end of today's practice because everyone gets out of the pool. Thank goodness.

"Get some rest tonight, ladies and germs," Coach announces through his bullhorn. "The bus for Carbondale leaves at three o'clock tomorrow afternoon from the rear of the building. Be on time. And be prepared to whup those pesky Catfish like they've never been whupped before."

"YEAH!!!!!!!!" The entire team throws their towels in the air and erupts into raucous sustained yelling and screaming. I can't quite make out what they're saying, but it appears to involve some form of killing or maiming. I get to my feet and walk shakily in the direction of the locker room.

"Hold on, Charlie," Coach Grubman calls. "You are officially on the swimming team, and that means you have a role to play at this meet, just like everyone else. You're going to be our mascot at the game tomorrow."

"Do I have to?"

"Yes," Coach says simply. "Here's your outfit." Coach hurls an enormous green felt Sardine costume at me. I catch it in my claws. It's got stupid-looking rubber fins, big dumb googly eyes, and silver sparkles all over it.

Oh no. Tell me this isn't happening. I can't wear this thing in public. I'm already strange-looking enough. I'll never live it down.

Coach hands me a few pieces of densely typed paper neatly stapled together. "These are your cheers. Learn them well, and perform them with plenty of pep. Don't slack off. Don't screw up." He turns on his heels and heads for his office.

According to Drinkwater's theory of relativity, tomorrow afternoon's meet will be starting in approximately twenty-five minutes and fifteen seconds. The countdown has begun.

16
JUST DESSERTS

"TURN OUT THE lights, Fred," my mom calls from the kitchen. "It's time."

My dad jumps up from the table and switches off the chandelier, plunging the dining room into relative darkness.

Light spills in from the hallway. I can still see Aunt Harriet grinning from ear to ear. It's her birthday today, and boy is she happy.

"Happy birthday to you, happy birthday . . ." My mom pushes open the door with her hip and enters the room. Her face glows from the light of fifty-three brightly burning candles. She proudly carries in the same high-calorie, sugar-laden, dense chocolate mocha fudge birthday cake she makes every year. Aunt Harriet loves it. I dare you to think of a dessert Aunt Harriet *doesn't* love. No wonder she's got a heart problem. Balthazar lies eagerly at her feet, waiting for a morsel of food to drop.

We all join in the song. My dad conducts with his fork. Dave throws a handful of confetti. Uncle Marvin toots his noisemaker enthusiastically. Aunt Harriet just stares at the cake longingly and licks her lips. "Make a wish, Harriet," my mom says as she carefully sets her creation down on the table. My aunt closes her eyes tightly and scrunches up her face for so long the candles have left a puddle of sticky wax over much of the cake by the time she gets around to blowing them out.

Aunt Harriet always takes forever to make her wish. I never knew why before. I do now. I bet she's wishing that Stanley's happy and safe. She must miss him a lot. I wish I could tell her how noble and brave he is. And how much he enjoys living under Crater Lake. But I can't. Not now, anyway. Not while he's still searching for the antidote. When I got home from school this afternoon, I put his dinner out behind the garage. His breakfast was gone. But last time I looked, dinner was still sitting there, untouched. I hope nothing happened to him.

"When are you planning to cut the cake, Doris?" Aunt Harriet asks as soon as she blows out the last candle. "I'm starving." Evidently being sad about her son hasn't affected her appetite.

"Soon, Harriet," my mom replies. "But first, in honor of *your* special day, I'd like everyone at the table to tell us about one special thing that happened to *them* today. You go first, Marv."

"Got my finger stuck in a bottle this morning," Uncle Marvin says cheerfully. "Boy, did that hurt."

"What's so special about that?" my dad asks.

"Got it out again!" He laughs and waves his bandaged finger.

"When do I get my cake?" Aunt Harriet persists.

"What about you, Charlie?" My mom ignores her sister. "Do you have anything special you'd like to tell us about?"

"Not really," I say.

"Charlie got chosen to be the team mascot at the big swimming meet tomorrow," Dave says proudly. "That sounds pretty special to me."

"How'd you find out, Dave?" I ask under my breath.

"I wasn't exactly planning on telling anyone."

"It's all over the school website, little bro. Sorry."

"That's amazing!" my mom exclaims. "Can you believe it, Fred! Team mascot? What an honor! Your father and I can't wait to come to Carbon-town or wherever you said the meet was and cheer you on, Charlie."

"We sure can't!" Dad exclaims. "This is wonderful. When do we leave?"

"Count me and Harriet in, folks." Uncle Marvin toots his noisemaker in my earflap. "We're so happy for you, Charlie!"

"It's really not such a big deal, guys," I protest. "Let's not get carried away here."

"Are you kidding?" My dad beams. "I wouldn't miss this for the world!"

Maybe you *wouldn't, Pop, but I sure would.*

"I'm ready for my cake now," my aunt says mournfully. "Is anybody listening?"

My mom is way too excited to pay attention to her sister. "We'll have to ask Mrs. Pagliuso to join us; I know she'll want to be there. And Fred, honey, make sure to check with your office to see who needs a ride to the swim meet. We'll probably have to rent one of those airport-type van thingies. I hope there's time." She gets up and clears the table. "Don't worry, Charlie, I'll start making decorative banners as soon as I'm done with the dishes."

I really wish my mom didn't make such a big deal out of everything. When Dave stopped wearing his retainer, she invited his entire freshman class over for a pizza party to celebrate. She bought Balthazar freeze-dried salmon treats and a shiny yellow raincoat when he graduated his obedience training course last year. He got special honors. Just like every other dog in his class who didn't bite the instructor.

"Cake, cake!" Aunt Harriet cries and reaches for the untouched dessert.

"My goodness, I was so excited about Charlie being team mascot, I nearly forgot the most important part of the meal." My mom snatches the cake out of Aunt Harriet's hands and starts slicing it into perfectly symmetrical wedges.

"For my wonderful sister on her fifty-third birthday." She puts the first piece on a plate and proudly presents it to my aunt. Aunt Harriet gobbles up every molecule of that piece of cake faster than you can say "if the birthday girl isn't careful, pretty soon she is not going to be able to get through the front door."

"You get the coffee, Fred, and I'll finish cutting the cake." My mom likes to run things almost as much as she likes to cook. "Dave and Charlie, you see who wants ice cream. Isn't this a wonderful evening!"

"I'd love another piece of that cake, Doris," Aunt Harriet says. "With a scoop of strawberry ice cream on the side."

"Can you wait until I've served the others, Sis?"

"No," Aunt Harriet says calmly. "I can't."

Just then, the doorbell rings.

"Fred, honey, can you see who that is?" Mom calls.

It's Principal Muchnick. I can smell him all the way from the front porch. Today he reminds me of Balthazar's breath mixed with chocolate chip cookies. It makes me feel a little hungry and a lot like I want to throw up.

Somehow I don't think he is here to congratulate me.

My mom doesn't even look up when my dad brings our principal and his flunky Doc Craverly into the room. "I'm afraid we're busy celebrating my sister's birthday tonight, gentlemen." She calmly finishes cutting the cake. "We don't have much time. I hope you understand.

What's going on?" My mom doesn't like Principal Muchnick very much. And she doesn't hide it very well, either.

Principal Muchnick clears his throat several times before he begins. "I'm here to discuss your son, Mr. and Mrs. Drinkwater."

We all look at him expectantly.

"I won't be long. I'm anxious to get to the bottom of this whole messy situation, as I'm sure are you."

"As far as we're concerned, there is no situation, Principal Muchnick," my mom says quietly and simply. "Messy or otherwise. Our son tells us he is innocent. We believe him. What else is there to discuss?" She passes the cake around the table.

"Uh . . . uh . . . uh . . . I see," Doc Craverly stammers. "Charlie is certainly a lovely . . . uh . . . boy . . . that's for sure . . . and you have every ra-ra-ra-reason to uh . . . believe . . . uh . . . whatever it is you want to believe . . . uh . . . ." Doc Craverly does not do well with confrontations. Or any other form of human interaction, for that matter.

"Butt out, Craverly," Principal Muchnick says ominously. Doc Craverly appears to shrivel like a dried prune. He hunches over, bites his lip, and stares at his shoes. My friends and I call this his "default" position.

"Doris, this dessert is outstanding!" Uncle Marvin beams. "Anyone who can bake this well deserves to have her own store. Don't you agree, Principal Muchnick?"

"I really never thought about it before, but . . . uh . . . yeah . . . sure." After an awkward pause, Principal Muchnick continues. "As you undoubtedly realize, Mrs. Drinkwater, there are two sides to every story. I hope you will do me the courtesy of listening to this discussion in the friendly and open-minded spirit with which it is intended. I assure you I will do the same."

Friendly and *open-minded* are not exactly words I would use to describe Principal Muchnick. *Stubborn, arrogant,* and *smelly* would be a lot more like it.

"I hope so," my mom says tersely.

"Yes . . . well . . . anyway . . ." Principal Muchnick says. "As you may or may not know, the police are no longer interested in pursuing the three robberies, as all plaintiffs have agreed to drop criminal charges. So it remains for Dr. Craverly and myself, on behalf of the school, to come to our own conclusion as to the guilt or innocence of your child."

Doc Craverly looks up cheerfully and seems to wink at me several times. I can't tell if he's trying to be friendly. Or has something in his eye. Or has simply developed an eye twitch. I try my best to ignore him.

"Just one more tiny little piece, Doris," Aunt Harriet whispers insistently. "And don't forget the strawberry ice cream, please."

"Not now, Harriet," my mom whispers back. "And what have you concluded?" she asks the principal, her voice rising.

Principal Muchnick pulls out a small, dog-eared yellow pad containing several pages of notes from his vest pocket. He begins to read aloud. He can't even look us in the eye. "Several factors have contributed to our belief that Charlie is indeed guilty of all three crimes."

"I thought this man was the school principal," Uncle Marvin comments. "Is he an experienced forensics professional?" Principal Muchnick gives Uncle Marvin a dirty look.

It's not exactly late-breaking news that Prinicipal Muchnick thinks I'm guilty. If someone steals a paper-clip, he calls me into his office the next morning and reads me the riot act.

"First and foremost," Principal Muchnick continues, "several additional eyewitnesses have come forward and placed your son at the scene of the Hollabird robbery, in addition to Mrs. Dieterly. Not only that, but we have studied the forensics of the case in great detail and can now prove beyond a reasonable . . ." He pauses while he turns the page and tries to find his place.

"I'm listening, Principal Muchnick," my mom says softly. "But I don't know for how much longer."

"My sentiments exactly," my dad mutters.

"Harumph," Aunt Harriet agrees, wiping the excess frosting from her extremely chocolaty lips.

Principal Muchnick finds his place and continues, unruffled, ". . . beyond a reasonable doubt that the robber was well over seven feet tall, and possessed unusual and highly advanced climbing skills. In addition, a number of clawlike marks were found at the scene of every crime, as well as . . ."

Uncle Marvin gets up and shakes his fist. I've never seen him so upset. "This is all circumstantial evidence at best, and we don't appreciate it one bit!"

"We understand you have a difficult job on your hands, Principal Muchnick," my dad says. "Somebody in this town has definitely done a lot of bad things, and if it's one of your students you're going to have to do something about it. But you've made a terrible mistake. It isn't our son you're looking for."

"Charlie Drinkwater never broke a rule in his life," my mom says.

Not exactly true, Mom, but thanks for standing up for me anyway.

"He is one of the most honorable people you'll ever meet," she goes on. "And if you thought twice about it, you'd realize what damage you're doing to this poor child with your unfounded accusations."

I wonder if she'd be saying this if she knew I snuck out last night and went swimming in Crater Lake without even a lifeguard present.

"He's innocent, Principal Muchnick," Dave says quietly.

"I appreciate your sentiments, everybody. But you're the boy's family. What else are you going to say?" Principal Muchnick motions to me. "Come over here, Charlie."

My mom squeezes my claw, and I get up from my place at the table and walk slowly over to the principal. I lean way down and he looks me right in the eye. He is so close to my snout I am becoming light-headed from the toxic smell of his cologne.

"I want you to listen to me very closely, Charlie. Doc Craverly and I are your advocates. We're on your side. We're here to help you." Principal Muchnick wants to help me about as much as I want to play defensive linebacker for the Stevenson Middle School football team. "But I only have so much patience."

He's not kidding. You could put all of Principal Muchnick's patience into a thimble and still have enough room left over for a couple of raisins and Craig Dieterly's heart.

"I'm offering you an opportunity, young man," Principal Muchnick continues. "The opportunity stands for the next twenty-four hours: confess to these thefts, and we can all move on and forget about your childish pranks. But if you remain silent, I will throw the book at you. Mandatory weekend study halls. Daily cleaning of the teachers' lounge. Weekly therapy sessions with Doc Craverly." Doc Craverly looks up gratefully. "I'll put you on the basketball team. It won't be pretty. And it will all be on your permanent transcript. Understand?"

Balthazar looks up at Principal Muchnick from

his treasured spot near Aunt Harriet's massive feet and growls protectively.

"I'm afraid I do," I say quietly. I'm supposed to lie and confess to something I didn't do so I won't get punished. What kind of a lesson is that for a principal to teach a kid?

"I'm going to have to ask you to leave now, Principal Muchnick," my mom says firmly. The corners of her mouth turn down and there is a big unhappy wrinkle etched in her forehead.

"You too, Doctor Craverly," my dad adds. "It's getting late. Charlie has a big day tomorrow. It's the big swim meet, as I'm sure you know."

We see our two visitors to the door in utter silence. The tension in the room is so thick you could cut it with the cake knife Aunt Harriet is currently licking clean of the chocolate.

My family tromps back to the dining room. I press one heavily hooded almond-shaped eye against the peephole and watch Principal Muchnick and Doc Craverly getting smaller and smaller as they head down the path.

If I ever become the principal of anything when I

grow up, please remind me never to act like Principal Muchnick.

"Aren't you going to watch Aunt Harriet unwrap her presents?" Dave calls. I notice a familiar-looking shadowy presence glide toward the front door, blending in effortlessly with the hedges by the side of the house.

"I'll be there in a minute!" I call back.

A thin, wraith-like figure wrapped in a black velvet cape steps gracefully onto the porch and stands alone, shivering in the wind. I open the door a crack. "What are you doing here, Mr. Arkady?"

"Usink only my powers of deduction, a leetle intuition, and a lot of scientific analysis, I seem to haff solved not vun but two great meesteries," he says quietly.

He leans in and speaks softly to me. I can smell his curiously scented lavender breath. "If my theory ees correct, I haff not only discovered who ees the Decatur robber, Charlie, but the identity of your mysterious friend vitt ull the difficulties, as vell. And, vunder uff vunders, they appear to be vun and the same."

Mr. Arkady's theories are, unfortunately, right on the money, as usual. He is so excited two red spots glow brightly on his normally sallow cheeks.

"Mr. Arkady, I don't mean to be disrespectful, but I don't really want to hear any more about your discovery. Because I don't want to have to lie to you, and no matter who you tell me it is, I will always deny it. I made my friend a promise. And I'm planning to keep it. I hope you understand, sir."

"You certainly are an honorable yunk lizard." Mr. Arkady stamps his velvet-slipper-covered feet on the porch to ward off the cold. "And as a fellow secret-keeper, I vill of course respect your vishes."

"I'm very grateful, Mr. Arkady." I wonder what

exactly Mr. Arkady knows. And how he knows it.

"But I must vorn you about vun tink, Charlie. I am ninety-nine percent certain that the person whose secret you are keepink vuss my stoodent nine years ago. He vuss a perfectly nice boy, but he had only a passink acvaintance vitt the truth."

I don't get it. Even if Stanley *was* Mr. Arkady's student, how does he know Stanley became a mutant dinosaur? I thought Stanley left town as soon as he transformed. There are missing pieces to this puzzle, and I really wish I knew what they were.

"The years have passed." Mr. Arkady's breath comes out in puffy white bursts. "Perhaps he ees older and viser now. Who knows? But eef I were you, I vould take effrytink he said vitt a grain of salt. Perhaps several grains. Udder than that, my leeps are sealed. Good luck beink team mascot. I vill be cheerink you on tomorrow." He swirls his cape, glides smoothly down the stairs, and disappears into the evening mist.

Why does Mr. Arkady want me to believe that Stanley isn't trustworthy? The Stanley that I know is brave. And kind. And honest. I'd trust Stanley with my life. I *did* trust Stanley with my life. Of course I nearly drowned. But that wasn't his fault. Or was it?

I hear the phone ringing in the distance.

"Charlie, it's for you!" my brother calls.

I race into the den and pick up the receiver quicker than you can say "the next time *your* mutant dinosaur cousin comes knocking, don't answer the door if you know what's good for you."

"It's Sam. Are you sitting down? Mrs. Pagliuso told Muchnick she saw you leaving Beautiful Bites right after the robbery the other day. Lucille and I . . . we thought you'd want to know."

"I'm not surprised. Principal Muchnick says a couple of other people saw me, too. He just left. He says he'll let me off easy if I confess to the crimes. If I don't, I'm in even worse trouble."

I hear a long sigh at the other end of the line. "What are you going to do?" Sam asks.

"Any suggestions?"

"Let's see . . . confess, get off easy, move on, put it all behind you. Or . . . don't confess, get into a lot of trouble for something you didn't do that will dog you for the rest of your life, and have your principal mad at you for your next five years. Let's see. After one or two nanoseconds of intense inner debate, I go with . . . confess. How about you, pal?"

"Sit tight and hope for a miracle."

"I figured. And worry about it all night, right?"

"Of course."

"You wouldn't be Charlie if you didn't. I mean that as a compliment. You'll do the right thing. My money's on you, pal. Good luck."

"Thanks. I'm going to need it."

17
OUT OF THE FRYING PAN

"COME ON, BALLY, it's getting late. Hold still." It's my turn to give the dog his evening walk, but he keeps dashing around the dining room, looking for stray crumbs. I guess he's still worked up from the birthday party.

By now Uncle Marvin and Aunt Harriet have gone home. Dave's helping Dad with the dishes. And Mom's in the den, letting out my dreaded Sardine outfit. I just tried it on. It would fit me pretty well if I didn't have legs, a tail, and a neck.

I finally manage to get Bally's leash and collar on him. He whines when I try to take him out the back door. "Be good, Bally. Please."

The second we're outside, I smell mutant dinosaur in the yard. So does Bally. He hides behind my legs and whimpers. "It's okay. Don't worry. It's just my cousin. He's very nice. He won't hurt you, Bally. Come on." We follow the smell to behind the garage. I'm practically dragging him at this point.

Stanley is sitting on the stump finishing his dinner. He looks up when he hears us coming. "Are you hungry, fella?" he asks Balthazar. My cousin reaches down and holds out a piece of chicken. Bally wanders over and sniffs it cautiously. In about two seconds flat he wolfs it down and begs for more. Feed that dog once and he's yours for life.

"Any luck finding the antidote?" I ask quietly.

Stanley gives me a long, hard look. "Yeah. Looks like my search is over, Charlie. I'll be heading for home soon. I guess it's safe to tell you now." My cousin closes the Tupperware container I left him and hands it back to me.

"That's . . . that's really great, Stanley." I am surprised to find myself getting choked up at the prospect of my cousin leaving.

"I couldn't have done it without you, Charlie," he says. "And I don't just mean the food. You kept my mission a secret. Because of you, thousands of innocent creatures will live."

Keeping Stanley's secret hasn't been easy. But it sure was worth it. I feel proud of Stanley. And not too bad about myself, either.

"Thanks, Stanley. I was wondering . . . now that you've found the antidote and you're going back to Crater Lake, do you think you could talk to Principal Muchnick? He still thinks I'm the robber, so if you could tell him it was you, I'd be really really grateful."

Stanley doesn't say a thing. He just sits there, staring into space and looking extremely upset. I wonder if he's sad about leaving. He didn't get to see his parents. Or any of his friends. He's probably wondering if he'll ever be back. I don't want to be insensitive, but if he doesn't go see Principal Muchnick before he goes, there is no way in the world anyone will ever believe I'm not the bad guy for the rest of my life.

"It's not like they can do anything to you," I explain. "You're not a student. Technically you're not even a resident. You're leaving town, anyway. What do you say, Stanley? Would you do that for me?"

"It's not that I wouldn't like to . . . uh . . . help you out . . . exactly . . . Charlie," he says. "But I really have to get back to the bottom of the lake. Waiting around for even another half hour could be a disaster . . . for all those . . . um . . . poor creatures. It's not that I wouldn't like to help you out . . . it's just . . ." He shrugs. "The timing stinks, that's all. I hope you understand."

I *don't* understand. The Stanley I know is thoughtful and kind. After all I've done for him, all I need is *one* thing and he won't do it? Is this what Mr. Arkady was trying to warn me about? Has some other Stanley taken my cousin's place, like in the highly underrated and extremely terrifying film *The Possession*?

"Sure," I say sadly. "Where's the antidote? Do you need me to lend you a suitcase or something to put it into? Is it very heavy?"

"I can't talk about it." He gets up and abruptly leaves without saying another word.

Something strange is definitely going on here. I can feel the uneasiness rumbling around in the bottom of my big round belly. Why is Stanley suddenly being so . . . different? What's wrong with this picture?

"Come back!" I start after Stanley, but just then I hear my mom's voice.

"Charlie!" my mom calls. "I'm ready for you to try on your Sardine costume!" I stop reluctantly and return to my house.

Mr. Arkady's words ring loudly in my earflaps. "Take everything he said with a grain of salt. Perhaps several grains."

I slip the costume over my head and look at myself in the mirror in the den. "What do you think?" Mom asks, beaming.

"I think you did a great job." I can't exactly tell her I look like a big, stuffed green olive with fins.

"Thanks, sweetie." She takes out her needles and pins, kneels down on her sewing cushion, and makes a few minor adjustments. "Your dad and I were talking, Charlie. We can't even imagine how difficult this whole thing must be for you. We hate to see you punished for something you didn't do. We want you to know that if you ever decide to take Prinicpal Muchnick up on his offer, we won't think less of you. And we would understand."

"Does this mean you want me to tell Principal Muchnick I was the robber, Mom?"

"Not at all," my mom explains. "We just want you to follow your heart. And whatever you think is right for you, we think so, too. That's all. Good night, honey."

How am I supposed to know what's right for me? I'm twelve. I just learned how to ride the city bus alone last year. I still require adult supervision to go to the movies. I can't even go to the dentist by myself.

Here's what I know: I know that nearly everyone on this planet thinks that I'm a liar and a thief. Even my neighbor Mrs. Pagliuso thinks I broke into Mr. Hollabird's store. Principal Muchnick is about to put a dark blot the size of Philadelphia on my official transcript. And the one creature who could stand up for me and get me out of all this trouble, my cousin Stanley, won't even bother coming to my defense because he has to rush to the bottom of the lake to bring a bunch of creatures the antidote to their disease.

I get into my bed and stare out the window. I watch the stars fade into a red glowing dawn that turns into an icy blue morning sky, and still I don't feel the slightest bit tired until my alarm goes off.

RINGGGGGGGGGGGGGGGGG!!!

And now all I want to do is go to sleep and pretend today isn't happening. According to Drinkwater's theory of relativity, the swimming meet will beginning in approximately five minutes and ten seconds.

I get out of bed, throw my Sardine costume into my backpack, and pray for a tornado or a hurricane to swoop down and take me away from this terrible, horrible, no good, very bad day.

Notes: _____

poor
Mia Farrow

WARNING:
Do **NOT** watch
"Rosemary's Baby"
again if you ever
plan to sleep through
the night

Send away
for fake
blood and
vampire fangs

avoid
lockets

Ah!
Ah!
Ah!

Why is
Swimming
so hard?!

REMINDER TO SELF:
pick up ten boxes
of fish food for
Dave's rare Egyptian
Mouth Breeders

Don't
eat fish
food

18
DON'T HOLD YOUR BREATH

IT SAYS ON the leaflet from Coach Grubman that Carbondale, Illinois, is an easy three-hour drive from Decatur. You could have fooled me. Sitting in the back of my mom's pickup, I could swear it's more like three hundred. I'm wet, I'm tired, and I have been bounced around so much I feel like loose change in a washing machine.

"We're almost there!" my dad calls from inside the cab.

"Great!" I look out from my perch in the back and see nothing but miles and miles of desolate plains and an occasional scraggly tree. Carbondale is famous for exactly three things: large coal deposits, really bad weather, and the best middle school swimming team in the central United States and possibly the universe.

We didn't have to rent a special airport van after all. The folks in my dad's office were too busy to come. And Mrs. Pagliuso had an appointment to have her hair done, so she stayed in town. Or at least that's what she told my mom. Since she thinks I robbed Mr. Hollabird, she probably didn't want to come.

Sam and Lucille are driving up with Sam's parents. So it's just me, my parents, Dave, Aunt Harriet, and Uncle Marvin. Usually the team mascot goes on the team bus. But I'm way too big to even get through the door.

We pull into the lot in front of Carbondale Middle School and park in the area marked MEMBERS OF THE SWIMMING TEAM AND THEIR FAMILIES ONLY. My mom hops out, carrying a big picnic hamper full of her best healthy snacks. She whips out her camera and snaps a picture of the sign. She is planning to create a scrapbook commemorating what she calls "the beginning of Charlie's adventures in competitive sports." In my opinion, being a mascot is neither competitive nor a sport.

"Won't this look great on the cover, Charlie?"

"Yeah, Mom. It's perfect." I grab on to the loading gate at the back of the truck with my claws and start dragging myself out.

"Oh, look! Aren't they cute?" Mom aims her camera at a couple of incredibly tough-looking members of the Carbondale swimming team heading toward the building. They have on beat-up motorcycle jackets that say CATFISH RULE on the front in large embroidered red letters. Across the back of each jacket a neon-yellow catfish wearing leather boots, brass knuckles, and a menacing sneer on its face sits astride the team motto ADVERSUS EXITUS OPTIO NON EST, which loosely translates from the Latin as "failure is not an option." Sam and Lucille and I took an extra credit Latin for beginners course last spring. The ancient Romans had about three million ways to let you know they were planning to kill you.

"Need a hand, son?" My dad holds on to my short stubby arm and helps me steady myself. I am so carsick I can barely walk in a straight line. I could upchuck at any moment. I am already dressed in the bottom part of my Sardine costume. My stiff, rubberized Sardine tail scrapes the ground behind me like a train wherever I go.

I guess this is what it must feel like to be a bride.

My real tail sticks out of a big hole my mom made in the side of my team mascot outfit. I carry my Sardine head in my claws. I slip it on and catch a glimpse of myself reflected in the glass doors to the gym. My painted-on smile looks very confident. My real face underneath is anxious and scared. I am dreading what Principal Muchnick will do to me when I don't confess to the crimes I didn't commit.

I just can't do it. It would make life so much easier if I could tell that lie, but I don't think I could live with myself if I did.

My mom pulls out her camera and points it at me. "For the scrapbook? I promise I won't get carried away."

I cock my fish head to one side and try to look peppy, but as she snaps my picture, all I can think about is Stanley deserting me in my hour of need, and how much I don't feel like jumping around in front of hundreds of people and screaming stupid pep cheers.

My parents, Dave, Aunt Harriet, and Uncle Marvin smile and wave their GO SARDINES pennants at me. Finally they all join the rest of the fans heading in to watch the meet.

As I turn to leave, I smell orange blossoms mixed with garlic and just a hint of rotten tomatoes. Principal Muchnick rushes over. Doc Craverly follows close behind.

"You have three hours and twenty-five minutes left to take advantage of my generous opportunity, Drinkwater. Here's a friendly little suggestion for you: COME TO YOUR SENSES AND CONFESS!"

The principal's cell phone rings. He presses it to his ear. "What? Are you sure? That's terrible, Coach Grubman. Yes. Uh-huh. I see." He hangs up, looking distracted. "Larry Wykoff missed the team bus this afternoon. Coach called the Wykoffs, but no one was home. And the boy isn't answering his cell phone. Have you seen him, Drinkwater?"

"No, sir." If I know Larry Wykoff, he got Velcroed to Rachel Klempner and can't tear himself away.

"Let's get going." Principal Muchnick grabs Doc Craverly by the arm and drags him into the building. I am about to follow when Mr. Arkady glides over to me.

"Goot evenink, yunk lizard," he says. "You're certainly lookink very interestink tonight." He waggles his pencil-thin eyebrows at me. "Vutt are you supposed to be dressed up as, son?"

"A Sardine, sir."

"Uff course you are. You look exactly like a sardine." He chuckles. "Only a teeny bit bigger."

"Mr. Arkady, what were you going to tell me about your student? I really need to know. My friend has left, and I have so many unanswered questions."

"Yunk lizard, I vill tell you everytink I know venn the time ees right and vee are alone." Mr. Arkady gestures to the crowd gathering in the parking lot, lowers his voice, and motions for me to bend down so he can whisper in my earflap. "I haff a leetle surprise vaiting for you after the meet," he says mysteriously. "In case you vurr tinkink uff rushink home tonight aftervurds."

"Can you give me a little hint, sir?"

"I'm afraid not," he says. "I vouldn't vant to ruin it for you." He swoops into the visitors' entrance to the gym.

Is Mr. Arkady going to surprise me with a critical piece of evidence supporting my innocence? Or a souvenir commemorating my debut as team mascot?

I open the big green door to the visiting team entrance marked MORITURI TE SALUTANT, which is Latin for "those who are about to die salute you." I'm beginning to wish I never took that Latin course in the first place.

I make my way up the long, cold concrete tunnel that leads to the changing area. My flippers slap noisily against the shiny cement floor. I push open the heavy metal door to the locker room. Row after row of giant fluorescent lights hang from the ceiling in heavy metal cages. A boisterous crowd of what appear to be dangerous felons mills around, cursing and pushing.

The Carbondale Catfish looked pretty threatening in the parking lot. Up close and half-dressed they look like maniacal killers out for their last night on the town before being sent to death row. The smell of chlorine is so strong it makes my eyes water and my large snout twitch.

As I make my way to the visitors' side of the locker room, Coach Grubman runs over to me. "There's been a change of plans, Drinkwater. Listen up."

"I'm all earflaps."

"This is no time for humor, Drinkwater. I just got a message from Larry Wykoff's dad. Larry's on his way to the emergency room in Farmingdale for some tests. Either he has an upset stomach from worrying about the meet and he'll be here in half an hour, or he's having an appendicitis attack. In which case you're going in for him in the four-hundred-meter freestyle."

"*What?!*" I exclaim so loudly half the locker room turns to see what's the matter.

"You heard me," Coach says. "If Wykoff can't make it, you're swimming in his place."

"What about Norm Swerling? He's really fast."

"He's already entered in three other races, Charlie. He's maxed out. So are all the other Sardines. You're the only one on the team who's legally allowed to take that slot."

"But . . . but . . ." I stammer. "I don't swim. I have performance anxiety. I'm not competitive. I fall apart under pressure. I haven't mastered any of the strokes. I could panic and drown. This is not a good idea, sir."

"I am well aware of your limitations in the water." Coach Grubman winds and rewinds his rubber band around his thumb and forefinger and taps his foot. "So let's just pray that Wykoff gets here in time. But if we don't hear from him soon, you can change out of that Sardine outfit and get into your bathing suit."

"I didn't even bring one!" I exclaim.

"Then you'll just have to wear the fish costume. Maybe it'll inspire you."

I am dizzy and weak at the thought of swimming

in an actual race in front of actual people. My enormous tongue is as dry as sandpaper and I am starting to lose feeling in the tips of my flippers. Early warning signs that a serious panic attack is waiting in the wings. I wander around the locker room aimlessly mumbling to myself. Larry Wykoff had better just show up soon. That's all I can say.

"Calling all Catfish and Sardines. Attention, please. The meet is about to begin." The announcement over the loudspeaker echoes around the white-tiled locker room. "Please assemble under the exit sign and prepare to enter the pool area."

Thirty-one swimmers, a gaggle of energetic cheerleaders, a small marching band, and one extremely anxious team mascot take their places.

"Eww! He bumped into me with his slimy tail," one of the Catfish whines as I pass him to get into position. "Where do I get a tetanus shot around here?"

Quicker than you can say "although there is a slim chance someone could develop salmonella from touching me, developing tetanus from exposure to my scales is impossible," the Carbondale marching band launches into a rousing chorus of "The Stars and Stripes Forever," and one by one we parade out of the locker room and out to greet our fans.

We are greeted by the ecstatic cheering of about five hundred or so fans in the bleachers. For one brief, shining moment, all thoughts of Larry Wykoff vanish and I understand what Dave sees in this athletic competition thing. Then the second the cheering stops, I go right back to feeling bleak and afraid.

We all gather around the pool and sing the national anthem. We put our right hands (or claws) over our hearts and begin: "O say can you see, by the dawn's early light, what so proudly we hailed at the twilight's last gleaming, whose broad stripes . . ."

I sneak a peek at the crowd. My parents and Dave sing proudly. So do Aunt Harriet and Uncle Marvin. I wonder if they're thinking about Stanley right now, and if he competed in any sports when he was my age. There's Sam and Lucille singing their hearts out on the end of the bench, and waving a pennant in their left hands in time to the music. Even Mr. Hollabird's here. His son, Grady, is swimming in the relay race today.

". . . o'er the land of the free, and the home of the brave." As the last note reverberates throughout the pool area, Coach Grubman comes over and taps me on the shoulder. "Hop to, Drinkwater. Get out there and do your stuff."

Since I have never actually seen a team mascot "do his stuff," the best I can do is run up and down the side of the pool, aimlessly waving my arms and kicking my legs. And yelling the one cheer I can remember from the pamphlet Coach Grubman gave me: "Sardines are smart and they're good for the heart. Catfish swim fast, but they won't last."

Performing in front of large groups of strangers usually makes me nervous, and tonight is no exception. Plus, added to the terrifying prospect of making a fool of myself, is the distinct possibility of death by drowning.

My small band of supportive friends and relatives joins in my chanting, but everybody else in the gym barely notices the eight-and-a-half-foot-tall green scaly creature in the Sardine costume hopping around the pool area like a hyperactive kangaroo. I'm not sure whether it is better to be noticed and mocked by your peers or ignored and forgotten entirely. Both sides of that penny are pretty discouraging.

Suddenly the Stevenson cheerleading squad runs in,

waving pom-poms and leaping around like a bunch of crazed Mexican jumping beans. Both Catfish and Sardines go wild with excitement. Grateful for the diversion, I skulk away and attempt to hide behind the bleachers.

Amy Armstrong, squad captain, leads everyone in a rousing cheer specially written for the occasion. "Fry those Catfish, put 'em on a platter, eat 'em all for dinner and you'll get a little fatter. Study little Catfish, learn learn learn, sizzle little Catfish, burn burn burn." Hundreds of audience members join in, enthusiastically stamping their feet.

By the end of the cheer, the team has formed a human pyramid, topped by Amy Armstrong. She leaps into the air, touches her toes with her outstretched fingers, and lands in the waiting arms of several of her minions, not a single wisp of hair out of place.

The cheerleading squad carries Amy Armstrong back to the girls' locker room on their shoulders, maintaining their perfect formation, while singing all three verses of our beloved school song, "Stevenson, Sweet Stevenson," in four-part harmony.

I keep checking out the crowd to see if Larry Wykoff has shown up yet, but there isn't a class clown in sight.

Even Rachel Klempner is conspicuously absent. I look around and spot Mr. Arkady sitting in the second row to one side, looking especially undead in the harsh gymnasium overhead lighting. He holds up a skinny thumb and smiles.

Doc Craverly sits to his right, looking at his watch and tapping his foot, while Principal Muchnick sits on the other side, nervously running his hands through his heavily pomaded hair.

An official wearing a crisp white-and-black striped uniform comes out and blows his whistle. Everyone quiets down immediately. "Places, please, for the two-hundred-meter butterfly stroke," he calls into his megaphone. "All lanes are clearly marked. Make sure you stay well within them."

I watch from the sidelines as swimmers from each team arrange themselves along the far end of the pool.

"On your marks. Get set. Go!" The official shoots his starting pistol and the swimmers catapult from the edge of the pool and into the water. They remain submerged way longer than you would have ever thought was humanly possible. I am already having sympathetic anxiety symptoms just watching them when suddenly they surface, hurtling forward like steroidal porpoises. A cheer goes up as the first swimmer finishes his ten laps. And then another one, and another. The pool goes quiet as everyone listens to the announcer with rapt attention.

"In third place, with a time of nine minutes and eleven seconds, let's hear it for Dirk Schlissel!" Banditos and One-Upsters scream their popular heads off. "In second place, with a terrific time of nine minutes and eight seconds, a big hand for Craig Dieterly." More sustained cheering and applause as Amy Armstrong careens out of the girls' locker room doing a spontaneous series of flips and cartwheels across the entire length of the pool and lands in a split right in front of the announcer.

"And in first place, with the near record-breaking time of nine minutes and three seconds, give it up, please, for the Catfish's own swimming sensation, Nelson Lutz."

The Sardine side of the room goes dead quiet as the Catfish pull out all the stops for their first blue ribbon of the night. The marching band plays a fanfare while Catfish cheerleaders do a dazzlingly complicated synchronized drill that makes Amy Armstrong and her team look like a bunch of preschoolers attending their first Mommy and Me class.

I guess Coach was thinking I would rise to the occasion when he made me team mascot. But the more the meet drags on, the more unhappy and anxious I get. My cheers are so uninspiring Coach Grubman suggests I concentrate instead on bringing towels to my fellow team members when I see their lips turning blue. The rest of the night is a blur of arms and legs and starter pistols and cheering.

With only a few races remaining, Coach Grubman hurries over to me. He whispers urgently in my earflap. "Mort Wykoff just called. He says Larry will be fine . . ."

"That's great, Coach!" I am so relieved I could cry.

"I'm not finished, Drinkwater. He says Larry will be fine as soon as he has his appendix removed. They're admitting him to the hospital as we speak. You're in the race after this one."

What I'm thinking is: *Noooooooooooooo!!! This can't be happening. I want to go HOOOOOOOME!!!*

What I say is: "I don't think I can do it, Coach. I'm not ready. Sign me up for a different meet. This one's a little too soon."

"You'll be okay, Drinkwater," Coach Grubman says. "Dig down deep and you'll find that inner athlete lurking inside you just waiting to come out. Believe me, it's in there somewhere. You just haven't found it yet."

I sure haven't. And I can't see how I'm going to find it in the next few minutes, either.

A cheer erupts from the bleachers. This race is over. I'm next. My heart beats wildly. My breath comes in quick shallow bursts. I'm light-headed and a little dizzy.

"And the winners are . . ."

I am losing sensation in my lower limbs. Coach Grubman holds my claw and leads me in the direction of the pool. "Don't pass out on me now, Drinkwater," he says. "Sardines trail by fifteen points. Let's go. Get into your starting position, Drinkwater. Now."

I feel faint. And nauseous.

"You're in lane six," Coach tells me.

I wander over to the edge of the pool in a daze and immediately forget where Coach told me to go, so I just stand in front of the first lane I see. Big mistake.

"You're in my space, Snake Eyes," Craig Dieterly barks. "Move over." He pushes me roughly out of the way. "I don't care what you do in your own lane, but stay away from mine. Understand?"

I nod weakly.

"Listen: don't screw up. We have a lot riding on this

race. The Schlissels and I can pull this whole thing off if you stay out of our way. So don't try anything funny."

"Okay . . . sure . . . no problem. I'm so cool with that, I'm cold."

What do I do now? With five hundred pairs of eyes watching, I can't exactly walk across the pool.

So many people have given me so many helpful hints about swimming, but in my hour of need, I can't seem to remember any of them. Surely there must be one useful gem buried in Mr. Miyagi's eight trillion pieces of unwanted advice. But if there is, I can't think of it now. All I can think of is drowning.

19

FULL SPEED AHEAD

I LOOK OUT at the water, moments before my first-ever swimming race, and suddenly plan B pops into my fevered brain. It's pretty radical. But I think it might work. Its main and only purpose will be to keep me from dying.

Here's is the plan: I am not going into the water. Period. The end. When the starting pistol goes off, I will grab my side, fall to the ground, and pretend to be having an appendicitis attack. By the time I get back from the hospital, the meet will be long over and I can go home alive.

It's a brilliant plan. Only (A) Aunt Harriet's weak heart will probably explode if she sees me having an appendicitis attack. And (B) this is exactly what is happening to Larry Wykoff right now, and that's why the plan occurred to me in the first place.

Right. Okay. So much for plan B.

"On your marks," the announcer begins. I stand, trembling, in front of lane six, praying for the race not to begin. I'm looking down at my flippers to make sure no part of me is protruding anywhere near Craig Dieterly's stupid space when I spot the dark piece of paper on the tiles, about a foot away from me. That's funny. Why would there be a piece of paper on the pool deck?

"Get set . . ."

Maybe if I hold my breath long enough, I can make myself faint. It's worth a try.

Wait a minute. I think that paper just moved. I must be mistaken. Paper doesn't move.

But bugs do. Terrifying water beetles that leap up at you with their giant, disgusting, gelatinous wings fluttering in your face do.

"Go!"

When the starter pistol goes off, the startled bug by

the side of the pool flutters its bat-like wings, shoots into the air like a speeding bullet, and crashes right into what passes for my face.

I shriek with terror. "ARGHHHHHHHHH!!!" And hurl myself into the water to get away from it. It never even occurs to me that I don't know how to swim.

The simple horrific fact of having an insect the size of a grapefruit attached to my face is currently occupying all the space in my brain devoted to "fear." There is simply no room left for anything else in there. I could probably give an impromptu address to Congress right now and fight an army of crazed mummies without even breaking a sweat, if I weren't swimming for my life in a pool in Carbondale, Illinois.

My thick, muscular legs propel me through the water like twin motorboats. My short, stumpy arms pound the surface like well-oiled pistons. I can think of nothing but fleeing from the enormous bug that clings to my snout until I finally shake it loose and its flies away to terrify some other swimmer.

I nearly crash into the wall in the shallow end, turn myself around, push off, head back into the deep end, push off the wall, start swimming back into the shallow end . . .

Hold on a minute. DID I SAY SWIMMING???

For a moment the realization that I am effortlessly speeding through the pool without a water wing in sight is so unnerving that I panic and start to sink. And that's when it happens: my gill slits begin to pulsate. The pulsating turns into a steady vibrating sensation. It feels like an army of cats purring softly inside my body.

My natural instincts are kicking in, just like Mr. Arkady said they would. I somehow know exactly what to do. I open my mouth and gulp in mouthfuls of water as fast as I can. Only instead of swallowing, I redirect it out through the slits in the sides of my neck, using muscles I never even dreamed I had. Row after row of gill tissue spring into action and suck the life-giving energy out of the H_2O and sends it coursing through my veins.

"A fish doesn't have to go to school to be a fish. It just knows." Coach Grubman, you were right! I lift my head up out of the water to thank him and hear my name being joyously shouted from every corner of the room. "Go, Charlie, go! Go, Charlie, go!" It's so thrilling that I complete my next four laps even quicker than my first four, barely aware of the other nine swimmers struggling in vain to keep up with me.

A roar goes up from the bleachers and I realize I have

completed my four hundred meters well ahead of the rest of the pack. I relax at the end of the pool, not even out of breath, and wait for my competition to complete their laps.

Craig Dieterly arrives first, gasping and wheezing, and immediately notices me waving to my fans. "What are you doing here, Broccoli Breath?" he pants. "You must have cheated. You can't be the winner. You don't even know how to swim."

"I do now," I say cheerfully.

While Craig Dieterly fumes, a Catfish swims to the finish, and the announcer yells into his bullhorn. "The race is officially over, folks. That was Mike Norsic in third place at six minutes flat. Craig Dieterly takes a speedy second with five minutes and forty-five seconds. And Charlie Drinkwater takes the blue ribbon with an astonishing world-record-breaking time of, will you listen to this folks, *five minutes and three seconds!* The Sardines win the meet in an amazing upset, narrowly beating the Carbondale Catfish by three points. Let's give it up for our new Central Illinois Champions, the Stevenson Middle School Sardines!"

Several hundred Sardine fans stand on their benches

and scream their hearts out as Amy Armstrong and her squad dance in from the sidelines. A happy Coach Grubman runs out and yells in my earflap, "What did I tell you, Drinkwater! I knew you could do it! From the first day I saw you. I knew it!" He notices Craig Dieterly glowering, gives him a swift "Nice job," and runs off to speak to the rest of the team. Sardine and Catfish fans stream into the pool area to get a closer look at me.

My relatives and friends climb down from the bleachers and fight their way through the crowd to congratulate me. "I was so excited I could hardly breathe, Charlie!" my mom calls.

"Me too, Mom!" I shout back.

"I'm so proud of you, son!" My dad beams. "Can you imagine? A world record? Harvard on an athletic scholarship, here we come!" He gives me a thumbs-up sign. And pretty soon every single person in that gym has their thumbs up—except Craig Dieterly, of course.

As Dave and a bunch of other upper-classmen attempt to hoist me up onto their shoulders, Principal Muchnick runs up to me ecstatically. "Congratulations! You did it! You won us the championship! Quiet, please, everyone!"

A hush falls over the crowd. Principal Muchnick continues, in a voice trembling with emotion, "In recognition of your astonishing achievement today I present you, Charles Drinkwater, with this humble token of our gratitude and admiration." He places a huge blue ribbon in my claws. "May you wear it in good health."

The crowd whistles and stamps and cheers. My mom rushes up to me with tears streaming down her face, pins the ribbon to my Sardine costume, and snaps a picture. I will never forget this moment as long as I live. I pinch myself to make sure I'm not dreaming.

"Hold on a minute," an angry voice shouts. "Has everybody lost their minds?"

The crowd grows quiet again. A tall, unhappy-looking gray-haired woman with enormous arms marches forward. "Since when do we give criminals blue ribbons and a pat on the back and forgive them their crimes because they win us state championships?" It's Mrs. Dieterly, of course. "Is that the lesson we want to teach our students, Principal Muchnick? I don't think so."

My mom looks like she could smack Craig's mom in the face. Principal Muchnick looks confused. A chorus of "Who is this woman?" echoes throughout the room.

Then another voice rings out. "Excuse me, every-

one." Stanley emerges from behind the bleachers. If you've never heard five hundred people gasp in unison, you should try it sometime. I'm here to tell you it's a pretty satisfying sound.

My enormous jaw drops even lower than Uncle Marvin's.

"May I have your attention, please?" he goes on. "I'd like to say a few words."

The crowd parts as he walks slowly forward.

"I'm Stanley O'Connor, everybody. I'm the other mutant dinosaur in the room. Hi, Mom. Hi, Dad." He waves to his parents. I watch carefully to make sure Aunt Harriet doesn't have a heart attack. She seems okay. She and Uncle Marvin rush up to their son and embrace him silently. Stanley hugs them back with all his might.

At last he breaks away. "I can't just walk away and let my cousin take the blame for everything I've done. I thought I could, but I can't. I know how much guts it took for you to dive into that pool and swim that race tonight, Charlie. You overcame your greatest fear. And if you can do it . . . then so can I. I hope."

Actually, it didn't take *that* much guts to get me into the pool. All it took was one extremely large palmetto bug. But what Stanley doesn't know won't hurt him.

The crowd whispers excitedly until Principal Muchnick calls for silence. "Quiet, everyone. I want to hear this." Stanley fidgets on his two large flippers, looks out at the crowd, takes a deep breath, and begins. "I broke into Dieterly's Delectable Denizens of the Deep and took their salmon. I stole my father's bag of used shoes, and the bread from the school cafeteria, and the dessert from Beautiful Bites. Yes, I was hungry. But what I did was wrong. I want you to know I acted on my own. My cousin Charlie had nothing to with any of this." Stanley pauses to take a deep breath. "I cannot tell you how good it feels to get this off my chest."

And I cannot tell you how relieved I am to be off the hook at last. You are looking at one happy fish.

Stanley comes over and looks me right in the eye. "You were kind to me when I needed you, Charlie. And I deserted you when *you* needed *me*. I'm really sorry, and I hope you accept my apology."

"Thank you, Stanley," I say quietly. "I do." It feels great when people apologize to you for what they've done, and nobody even has to make them.

Then Rachel Klempner pipes up. "Attention, please! I bring you a message from the most wonderful guy in the world, Larry Wykoff!"

Everybody turns to see who the strangely enthusiastic girl is.

"He told me to tell you how proud he is of each and every one of you here tonight. And he asked that we Sardines give a great big cheer to all you Catfish who swam so hard, and were such good sports. Hip hip HOORAY!!!

"Larry and I wanted to say something especially to

you, Charlie. Because we admire and respect you so very much."

Rachel Klempner and Larry Wykoff respect me about as much as Moe and Curly respect Larry. Maybe a little less.

"Larry heard about your amazing record tonight, Charlie Drinkwater, and he specifically wanted me to tell you he's not at all surprised at how well you did. We both have the utmost respect for you. You have come so far in such a short time. You're our hero and you always will be." Rachel Klempner has actually moved herself to tears during this last part.

I would bet you three billion dollars that Larry Wykoff didn't tell her to say anything. She just made it all up. She doesn't mean a word of it. She never does. As the crowd breaks up the loudspeaker clicks on:

"Please exit in an orderly fashion. No running in the parking lot. And please, drive safely. The life you save may be your own."

At least that's an announcement you can trust.

Stanley joins us in the corridor and we make our way to the parking lot. Mr. Arkady catches up to us just as we reach my mom's truck. "Vell done, Charlie."

"Thanks," I reply.

"I vuss impressed vitt your performance as vell, Stanley. You told the truth, the whole truth, and nuttink but."

"I haven't had a lot of practice at that sort of thing." Stanley and I hoist ourselves into the back of the truck.

"I trust you vill heff many more opportunities for tellink the truth," my science teacher says.

"I'm really glad you made Stanley come to the swimming meet, Mr. Arkady. It meant a lot to me. How'd you do it?"

"Vell, Charlie, last night venn I came to see you, I noticed garbage scattered everywhere behind your garage. And several sets of flipper-prints. Eet deedn't take a genius to know you vurr feeding Stanley. So after I left you, I vaited in the shadows for heem to come and see you. And venn *he* left I had a leetle visit uff my own vitt your cousin in your backyard. I deedn't *make* him come to the meet, Charlie. I merely *suggested* he come in case he changed his mind about confessink."

"Well, whatever you did, I'm glad you did it," I say.

"Me too, Mr. Arkady," Stanley adds.

"Good night, Mr. Arkady!" my mom calls as she and the rest of my family climb into the truck.

Mr. Arkady smiles a contented smile and glides away.

Just as she's about to pull away, Mr. Hollabird pokes his head in the window. "I owe you an apology, Mrs. Drinkwater."

"Yes, you do," my mom replies simply.

"I've been foolish and stubborn and wrong."

Mom just sighs and shakes her head.

"I don't blame you for being upset, Mrs. Drinkwater. If someone had accused my son, Grady, of crimes he didn't commit, I'd be upset, too."

"I appreciate your apology, Mr. Hollabird. But I really have to go now." My mom starts the engine. "It's been a long day." The old truck lurches forward.

I stick my long neck through the back window and whisper into her ear. "Don't be so stubborn, Mom. He's practically groveling. If I can forgive him, why can't you?"

Mr. Hollabird jogs alongside us. "I hope you'll consider bringing your six favorite healthy desserts to our charity bake-off next week, Mrs. Drinkwater. I'd be honored if you would. I've heard wonderful things about your gluten-free, reduced-calorie, soy protein brownies."

"He's really sorry, Mom," I say softly. "Please say yes. Don't be such a Grinch."

"I'll have to think about it," she says.

"Please do," Mr. Hollabird says gratefully. "Beautiful Bites could really use a person like you on the team!" He keeps on jogging.

My mom keeps driving. And then she looks out the window at Mr. Hollabird, beaming. "What day is the bake-off?"

HOORAY! She just gave in. "Good work, Mom."

"Wednesday!" Mr. Hollabird stands by the side of the road, holding his side with one hand, and waving with the other as we roar off. Soon he is just a speck in the distance. I lean back and smile. What started out to be a terrible, horrible, no-good, very bad day in November is turning out to be a pretty okay day after all.

20

END OF THE RAINBOW

"STANLEY, THERE'S ONE thing I'm still wondering," I say. "*Why* wouldn't you tell Principal Muchnick I was innocent last night?"

"I was afraid to let him see me. You have to realize that until tonight I've never let *any human* see me. Except my mom and dad. I couldn't take the rejection. *You're* the brave mutant dinosaur in the family, Charlie. Not me."

"No, Stanley, you both are," Aunt Harriet says. "And now I'm losing you again. I can't bear it." She blows her nose so loudly that Balthazar whines and covers his ears.

"There, there, Harriet." Uncle Marvin takes her in his arms.

My family is gathered at the edge of Crater Lake, saying our good-byes to Stanley. It's nearly midnight. There isn't a cloud in the sky. The screech owls are screeching. The pine trees sway gently in the wind. It's just like a scene from *Night of the Living Dead*, only without the living dead.

"You're not losing me, Mom," Stanley explains. "I just have to go back down and straighten out a couple of things, and . . . no." Stanley stops himself. "It's going to be harder than that. I'm going to have to apologize. And return the money that I borrowed and then . . . no." He stops himself and starts again. "I *stole* that money. And it's going to take me a while to pay it back. But I will. Just like I'll get used to telling the truth. And after I do that, I'll be back, guys. I promise." He takes a couple of steps into the lake.

"Is that why you *really* left Crater Lake and came to Decatur, Stanley?" I ask. "Because you owed other creatures money? You weren't on a mission to save our relatives from extinction?"

"Afraid not, cuz." Stanley hangs his head. "There isn't any disease, and there isn't any antidote either. And I never taught anyone to swim, and Aunt Harriet doesn't have a heart problem. Do you hate me?"

I have to think about that for a moment. Am I glad Stanley lied to me and got me in trouble and made my life miserable? Of course not. Do I understand why he did it? I think so.

"No," I say. "I don't hate you, Stanley."

"I'm glad."

Stanley takes a few more steps into the lake until the water is just about up to his neck. You can see his reflection in the moonlit surface like in *Creature from the Black Lagoon* when the creature abducts Dr. Reed's girlfriend, Kay Lawrence, and takes her to his lair.

"We'll miss you, Stanley," Dave says.

"Bye, Stanley." I hold up my claw. "I'm glad I got to know you."

"Me too, cuz." Stanley takes one last step and sinks slowly out of sight.

We all watch quietly until the last ripple stops rippling. And then we start the long walk home.

"What was it like when Stanley transformed, Uncle

Marvin?" I break the silence. "Were you scared?"

"Pretty much. How about you, Harriet?"

"I was . . . concerned . . . for Stanley. He was always such a sensitive child. Let's just say it was a lot to deal with and leave it at that." Aunt Harriet glances nervously at my mom, who returns the look and glances at my dad. And then ominous silence.

Something's up. I have stumbled onto an undercurrent of something. But I'm not sure what.

"Didn't Stanley run away?" Dave asks innocently. "I was only six or seven at the time, but I thought I remembered something about him running away."

Everybody turns to my brother and glares. And still nobody speaks.

"Come on," I say. "Somebody knows something here and they're not saying. If Stanley could learn to tell the truth . . . couldn't we?"

My mom speaks reluctantly. "When Stanley mutated . . . he hid in the basement and refused to go to school. He was ashamed. He wouldn't let anyone outside the family see him. He finally agreed to speak with his science teacher, but even Mr. Arkady couldn't think of anything to do."

Aunt Harriet picks up the story. "So we pledged Mr. Arkady to secrecy and told everybody that Stanley had gone to live with his uncle in Ohio. We never told anyone else that he transformed into a creature."

"He didn't really have an uncle in Ohio," Uncle Marvin continues. "Instead Stanley ran away to the bottom of Crater Lake because he couldn't cope with being different."

So *that's* the big secret that Mr. Arkady has been hiding all these years. And that's how come he knew so much about my cousin. The pieces of the puzzle are all fitting neatly into place.

"You all knew my cousin turned into a mutant dinosaur all this time, and you never told me about it? When I transformed, it would have been nice to know I wasn't the only one."

"We didn't want you getting ideas, Charlie," my dad replies. "What if you decided to run away, too? What would we have done then?"

"It's really hard to keep secrets," I say. "There are so many things you have to remember. Do you think maybe we could all start telling the truth around here, guys?"

"Umm." Mom goes first. "Some of my vegan cookies have a little butter in them."

Aunt Harriet picks up the ball. "I keep several birthday cakes at home in the freezer and eat them from time to time, and I don't even defrost them."

"I hate the hat you gave me for my birthday, Doris. I gave it to the Salvation Army. I didn't really leave it at the office," my dad confesses.

"Stanley gave me swimming lessons in Crater Lake last night after everybody was asleep," I say quickly and quietly.

"Charlie Drinkwater! I'm going to pretend I didn't hear that one." My mom holds her hands over her ears.

"I don't have any secrets," Dave admits. "That's my secret."

The dirt path turns into sidewalk. The pine trees thin out to the occasional stubby cedar. Aunt Harriet and Uncle Marvin turn left at Maple. My parents, Dave, Balthazar, and I head straight for Lonesome Lane.

So that's my story. I didn't exactly conquer my greatest fear. But I dealt with it. With the help of a creepy palmetto bug, I turned it into a friend instead of an enemy. Thank you, Doc Craverly. Like my dad says, even a stopped clock is right twice a day. This week, swimming. Maybe next week . . . tapioca pudding! Who knows?

"Hey, look at that!" As we approach the house, Dave points above our heads. A tiny silver dot streaks across the sky.

"What do you think that is, Dave?" Dad asks.

"Probably a meteor from outer space hurtling toward earth."

"Stop it, Dave," Mom says. "You're scaring your little brother."

"That's what big brothers are for." He smiles.

I should never have told him I was afraid of meteors. He's always doing this.

"Last one in is a rotten pumpkin!" Dad opens the front door. Balthazar strains at his leash and whines.

"What's the matter with Bally?" Mom asks.

"He didn't do his business." I look at my brother. "Your turn, Dave."

"Uh-uh. No. Forget it," Dave says. "I am not taking that animal out for another walk. Over my dead body."

Guess what? Dave walks Balthazar again. And by the time he gets home, I almost don't hear him come into the room. I am too busy thinking about conquering my next fear. And breaking a world record. And wondering how Stanley is doing. And pretty soon I am pretending not to notice the fly buzzing over my head. And wondering whether maybe it is a tsetse fly that could bite you and kill you. Or whether it is a regular ordinary housefly.

And then I turn off my mind and do what comes naturally: I fall asleep.

TURN THE PAGE
FOR A SAMPLE OF ANOTHER
CHARLIE ADVENTURE!

PROLOGUE

THIS IS A STORY about how something truly extraordinary can happen to the most ordinary of people (which I happen to be). Even if you lived in Decatur, Illinois (where I actually live), and were twelve years old (which I am), and the craziest thing you had ever done in your life was watch *Return of the Jedi* five times in one day (which I actually did when I was nine)—even then, something truly extraordinary could happen to you.

Everything I am about to tell you is true. It's not "loosely based on," or "suggested by," or anything even remotely like that. I would swear on the lives of my seven turtles, but you probably wouldn't believe me anyway. I am still having a hard time believing it myself, and it happened to me.

Let me put it to you this way: if you suddenly became invisible and could fly and were able to teleport yourself to a planet inhabited by talking cheese balls over twelve trillion light-years away in less time than it takes to wash your hands, it wouldn't even come close to what I am about to tell you.

Before we go any further, here are a few things you should know about me: I am a seventh-grade student at Stevenson Middle School, grades five through eight. I am not exactly the most popular kid in my grade. Translation: if you rated my popularity on a scale of one to ten with one being the lowest and ten being the highest, it would be zero. Does that bother me? What do *you* think.

My big brother, Dave, is a senior at Stevenson Upper School, grades nine through twelve. He is so popular it hurts. He is tall, gets invited to everything, and was recently voted Most Likely to Succeed in the annual yearbook poll.

Dave is Chief Justice of the Student Court. He has

three girlfriends. Plus he got early acceptance to his favorite college (Michigan State). And did I mention that he's really nice, isn't at all stuck-up, and is great at every sport known to man plus a few you have probably never even heard of like "Frisbee golf" and "water polo"?

Well, I'm only twelve, so I'm not all that interested in three girlfriends and early acceptance to college at this point. But other than that, do I wish I could be more like Dave? Let me put it to you this way: *duh*.

Craig Dieterly is my nemesis. His hobbies are burping, dropping water bombs, and making my life miserable. He is the president of the seventh grade (he ran on a platform of "Vote for Me or I'll Hurt You"). He's captain of everything. Football. Baseball. Soccer. The world. You name it. He is six feet three inches tall and weighs about thirty million pounds. If his brain were a state it would be Rhode Island.

Craig Dieterly has been picking on me since the day I entered Stevenson Lower School in prekindergarten. He used to terrorize me on the playground. Once he wouldn't let me get off the whirl-and-twirl and kept spinning me around until I threw up. Another time, in the sandbox, he stole my pail and shovel and refused to give them back until the head of the entire Stevenson Lower School, pre-kindergarten through grade four, threatened to call the police.

In homeroom our desks are in alphabetical order. My last name happens to start with a "D." It's Drinkwater. Don't laugh. So every morning I have to sit next to this Craig Dieterly guy. We have a deal: I sharpen his pencils and do his math homework, and he doesn't steal my lunch money. Unless he feels like it. He refers to me as "Snow White's little-known eighth dwarf, 'Brainy,'" when he refers to me as anything.

In case you were wondering, my full name is Charles Elmer Drinkwater. (What were my parents thinking?) I hate my middle name so much even my best friends don't know what it is. **PLEASE DO NOT TELL ANYONE.** When I was eight I tried to have it legally removed from my birth certificate, but you're not allowed to alter official records until you're over eighteen. I checked. If Craig Dieterly ever finds out my middle name is Elmer, I will have to relocate to another solar system.

Did I mention that my voice hasn't even begun to change, so when I answer the phone people still say, "Can

I talk to your mother, little girl?" Embarrassing but true.

Oh, and I don't do sports. Call me crazy, but I try to avoid getting squished or maimed or humiliated whenever possible. Last year Principal Muchnick made a rule that all middle school boys had to join the middle-school football team. I told him it was my constitutional right to refuse to play a sport that could cause premature death.

Principal Muchnick doesn't like it when students disagree with him. He told me to quit bellyaching and join the team. He said it would make a man out of me. I told him I thought I was a little small to play football.

That is a gross understatement. There are beagles I know that weigh more than I did. In fourth grade I nearly blew away in a strong wind. Both feet were off the ground and I was halfway down the block by the time I managed to grab hold of a fire hydrant. Alice Pincus, the littlest girl in my class? Last year Norm Swerling dared her to pick me up and carry me to the end of the hallway outside of language lab. She didn't even break a sweat.

Needless to say, Principal Muchnick prevailed and I joined the team. My father had to order custom-made shoulder pads for me because they didn't come in my size.

In the first quarter of my first and last game I caught the ball by mistake and three defensive linebackers the size of refrigerators came running after me. I was so scared I fainted before they could tackle me, and Nurse Nancy had to give me smelling salts and carry me to her office to recover. Try living that one down.

Mom always said I should drink my milk, take my vitamins, and be patient. She promised me that I would eventually go through some kind of "magical transfor-

mation" and sprout like a weed and I wouldn't have to get my clothes in the little boys' department anymore. Guess what? Mom was right.

My story begins at three o'clock in the morning one cold and windy Monday in October. It is not for the faint of heart. Don't say I didn't warn you.

Notes:

Remember to give Craig Dieterly my lunch money if I want to live to see thirteen.

Grr! Yargh!

Pew! pew!

Ask Mrs. Adams why she only gave me a 96% on my paper.

I can help, Amy

My hero!

Ask Amy Armstrong if she needs help with her math homework.

1
THE JOURNEY BEGINS

IT'S THE MIDDLE of the night. I awake scream-ing in a sweaty, heart-stopping panic, gasping for breath, legs tangled in the sheets. I've had this nightmare before. Seven times in the past seven days, but who's counting. Dave mumbles "shut up" from his bed on the other side of the room and goes back to sleep faster than you can say "little brothers are a serious pain in the butt."

The dream always begins the same way. First my face turns green. Then I get scales all over my body. Next my toes transform into hideous, long, webbed things that taper into razor-sharp toenails. By the time the gill slits begin to form at the base of my ever-lengthening neck, I scream and wake up. Just your plain old recurring "I'm turning into the Creature from the Black Lagoon" dream.

Creature happens to be my favorite monster movie. The scene where the creature skulks around in his lagoon and watches mild-mannered Dr. Reed's beautiful girlfriend, Kay Lawrence, swimming just above his head is a classic. I give it eleven goose bumps out of a possible ten on the fear-o-meter. It is an official "Monsterpiece" in my book.

My dad says that if you have a vivid imagination and you go around watching scary movies before you go to bed, you have to be prepared for a certain number of bloodcurdling nightmares. It comes with the territory.

But this isn't my imagination. I know it. Just as sure as I know that E equals mc^2. So I drag myself out of my nice warm bed, quietly tiptoe over to the bathroom, doing my best not to wake Dave again, and try to tell myself that the clammy sense of dread I'm experiencing is from staying up too late watching *Poltergeist* and *Rosemary's Baby*.

Still shaking, I peer into the mirror. The circles under my eyes are definitely darker. But then, if you woke up in the middle of the night for the last seven days in a row, the circles under your eyes would be pretty dark, too. And my skin *has* taken on an alarming greenish caste. After careful scrutiny, I chalk it up to the fluorescent bathroom lighting and shuffle back to bed.

I remind myself that it was just a dream. But try as I might, I am unable to shake the feeling that life as I know it is about to come to an end.

2
IT'S NOT THAT EASY BEING GREEN

MY SCIENCE TEACHER, Mr. Arkady, stands in front of first-period science class and slowly writes the word HERPETOLOGY in big script letters across the blackboard. He looks and sounds exactly like a vampire. If I didn't know for 100 percent certain that Bela Lugosi was dead (I saw his grave in a documentary on the SyFy channel once), I would swear he had returned as a Stevenson Middle School teacher and taken over Mr. Arkady's body.

I asked my mom to get me transferred out of his section when school started this year because I didn't want to have a vampire for a teacher, but she just said I'd have to deal with it. I'm glad she made me, because he turned out to be one of my favorite teachers. (But I still wouldn't want to run into him in a deserted alley on a dark and stormy night.)

"Who knows vut that vurd means? Hands, please," he says, gliding back to his desk, humming a haunting melody, and carrying an ancient leather-bound notebook in his long bony fingers. There is a rumor floating around that Mr. Arkady keeps a running total in there of all the people whose blood he has sucked and turned into vampires, along with their vital statistics—height, weight, hair color, and exact moment of death (or undeath).

In my opinion, Mr. Arkady is a really great teacher. He has a good sense of humor, he encourages us to think on our own, and he always has time to talk to us about our problems. The fact that small children run screaming at the sight of him is not his fault.

"Surely somebody knows the meaning of that vurd."

A sea of blank faces stares back at him.

I know exactly what herpetology means (it's sort of a hobby of mine, actually), but I am much too busy staring at my hand to raise it. It's all dry and cracked looking.

And it has the same dull greenish tinge that it had in my nightmare last night. Hmm.

Lucille Strang, one of my best friends, raises her hand. Lucille knows the answer to just about any question you could think of asking and isn't bothered one bit by the fact that the rest of the class thinks she's a know-it-all. Because basically she does know it all.

Lucille has an IQ of about forty million and a mouth so jam-packed with braces that it's virtually impossible for her to get through a metal detector without an intervention from the National Guard. At six feet one and a half inches, she is the tallest girl in the entire Stevenson School District, grades prekindergarten through twelve, and, as far as I can see, the tallest girl in all of Decatur, Illinois, population 76,122.

At Stevenson Middle School if you're a boy and you're really tall, you get three extra points on your popularity scorecard. If you're a girl it's at least ten points against you. If you're Lucille and your hobbies are experimenting with fruit flies, playing with your ferrets, and learning about the space-time continuum, take off another fifteen.

What's up with my feet? They're all puffy and

swollen. They crowd the sides of my size-three sneakers like they're trying to escape. This is not a good feeling.

"Students, please, vair did you hide your brains today?" Mr. Arkady says, drawing himself up to his fullest height and hunching his shoulders like he's adjusting his bat wings before swooping down on an unsuspecting victim. "Surely somevun besides Miss Strang knows vut a herpetologist is."

Sam Endervelt raises his hand. He's my other best friend. It's a small subset. He's kind of round and really, really pale. He sort of looks like Gomez from *The Addams Family* except he's too young to have a mustache. A lot of people are scared off by Sam's freaky, ultralong dyed purple hair. He's sort of pre-Goth. Like he's not all the way there yet, but he paints his fingernails black and wears a fake nose ring. He also sings soprano in the school chorus because even though he's six months older than I am his voice hasn't changed yet, either. He's harmless. I swear.

If I'm a geek, Sam's an off-the-charts supergeek. He says the number on his popularity scorecard is so low it's unlisted. Sam knows a lot about popularity scorecards. He should. He invented them. There's no actual card or anything. As Sam is quick to explain to anyone who will listen, it's a humorous way of demystifying popularity that makes it seem silly and unimportant. Guess what? It doesn't work. Uh-oh. My calves are starting to tingle. Like when you've been sitting in one position for too long and your legs are about to fall asleep. Only I haven't been sitting in one position for too long. Did I mention that my tongue is also up to something funny? It feels thick and lumpy and dry.

Sam pokes me in the back. "What's with your neck, pal?" he whispers. "It looks like it's got mold growing all over it."

"I have no idea," I whisper frantically.

"I guess that's what happens when you don't wash behind your ears." He chuckles. For a moment I wonder whether I'm getting some kind of weird cosmic payback for my inattention to personal hygiene. "You're starting to look like Jeff Goldblum in *The Fly*."

"If you ver a herpetologist . . ." Mr. Arkady continues as he scans the room for someone to call on. (He's actually 35 percent less likely to call on you if you raise your hand. I keep track of stuff like that.) "Vut ting vood you know a lot about . . . uh . . . Amy?"

Amy Armstrong, the most popular girl in Stevenson Middle School, grades five through eight, and possibly the universe, looks up distractedly. "Gee, I'm drawing a blank."

"Perhaps if you and Rachel Klempner paid as much attention to vut I am sayink as you do to the notes you are passing to each udder, maybe you vood know vut is goink on in this class."

Amy Armstrong gives Mr. Arkady a dirty look.

Rachel Klempner, on the other hand, smiles cheerfully, like Mr. Arkady has just paid her a great compliment. She pretends to like everybody to their faces, and then she goes around behind their backs and says terrible things about them. In fifth grade she started a rumor that Lucille and Sam and I had a contagious disease that caused us all to have really bad hair. No one would sit next to us for weeks.

Rachel has been going out with Larry Wykoff since last year. She wears this stupid ring he gave her to commemorate the day he first texted her. It looks like it came out of a Cracker Jack box, and it's made out of plastic. Once it got lost during gym period, and she almost had a nervous breakdown and had to be sent to Nurse Nancy's office.

Rachel and Amy are members of the One-Upsters, a seventh-grade clique dedicated to the proposition that all middle-school girls are definitely *not* created equal, and the ones with better clothes and even better hair really are . . . well . . . better.

One-Upsters can usually be found hanging with Banditoes, their male counterparts. Banditoes, like Craig Dieterly and Larry Wykoff, are great at sports, care deeply about their sneakers, and tend to have fewer pimples than everybody else. Banditoes and One-Upsters wouldn't be caught dead talking to Mainframe weirdoes. Namely Lucille, Sam, and me.

We Mainframes are happy to hang with anybody who is willing to hang with us. Nobody's exactly lining up. Well, actually, on the first day of school this year, Alice Pincus asked if she could be a Mainframe, and of course we said yes because (A) we think it's rude to reject people who want to join your clique. And (B) nobody ever wants to and it's pretty embarrassing having a clique with only three people in it. But after she hung with us for a few days, Alice Pincus ditched us and went on the waiting list to become a One-Upster.

"Take a vild guess, Miss Armstrong." Mr. Arkady

isn't about to give up. "Vut does a herpetologist do?"

What's up with my shoulders and my neck? It's like my insides are rearranging themselves. It doesn't exactly hurt. But I wouldn't recommend it, either. I ache everywhere. I am definitely coming down with something. If this continues I will have to go see Nurse Nancy for sure.

"I think I know!" Amy says excitedly, like for once in her life she might actually have the answer to a question besides "What time does the party start?"

"I believe a herbologist is someone who knows a lot about different kinds of cosmetics. And herbs." Amy smiles beguilingly at Mr. Arkady, then goes back to reading Rachel's note.

"It's *herp*etologist, Miss Armstrong." Mr. Arkady is clearly not beguiled in the least.

Suddenly I get such a severe cramp in my right arm that I start waving it around in the air.

"Mr. Drinkvater, vill you please put us out of our misery and tell us in vut field you vood be an expert if you ver a herpetologist?"

"I would know all about amphibians and reptiles, like snakes and turtles and lizards," I blurt out, lowering my right arm and massaging it with my left. I really do feel sore. I hope I'm not getting the flu. Halloween is Friday. It's my favorite holiday, and I don't want to miss it. Last year I went as Frankenstein. This year I'm either going as the Invisible Man or the Mummy.

"Derivation, if you please, Mr. Drinkvater," Mr. Arkady asks.

"The word 'herpetologist' comes from the Greek word 'herpeton,' which means things that crawl," I say as I hold the back of my hand to my forehead to see if I'm running a fever. I don't feel warm. I feel cold and clammy. "Like Herman, for example."

I glance over at Herman the iguana, who usually spends his time lazing in the corner of his cage under the relaxing glow of his basking lamp. He suddenly begins to pace around his little enclosure like a convicted felon trying to break out of the slammer.

Herman's looking over at me like he's just laid eyes on a long-lost friend. He makes happy little chirping sounds and jumps up and down trying to attract my attention. *Sit, Herman. Stay.*